REGINALD BIRCH—HIS BOOK

Reginald Birch
— His Book

Edited by Elisabeth B. Hamilton

A SELECTION OF STORIES AND POEMS
WITH REPRODUCTIONS OF THE ORIGINAL ILLUSTRATIONS
MADE FROM 1886 TO 1938 BY REGINALD BIRCH

HARCOURT, BRACE AND COMPANY

NEW YORK

I

To the Children

of Yesterday, Today, and Tomorrow

When I was a little boy I wanted to be a sailor, later an actor. Strangely I've been both, sailing over a far bigger ocean than you can find charted on any map. On the ship there was a theatre where, storm or shine, many plays were produced to an unseen audience—little but very big, and I not only acted all the parts in all the plays, including the animals, but was scene painter, property man, and general Director. Now that the voyage is almost over and we are nearing Port, this book will be cast overboard in the hope that it will serve as an anchor to hold my ship of dreams snug and secure in the safe harbor of your hearts.

Reginald Birch

ACKNOWLEDGMENTS

FOR permission to reprint the stories and poems in this book, the editor thanks the authors and the publishers who are holders of the copyrights. This indebtedness is hereby definitely acknowledged and recorded:

TO D. APPLETON-CENTURY COMPANY for the selection from *Master Skylark* by John Bennett, and for the following stories and poems which appeared in *St. Nicholas Magazine* between the years 1893 and 1902: *The Scribe of Durley* by Virginia Woodward Cloud, *A Yarn of Sailor Ben's* by Tudor Jenks, *A Day with Baby* by Malcolm Douglas, *The Grumpity Man, Wishes* by Florence E. Pratt, *The Dragon and the Dragoon* by Tudor Jenks, *What the Lord High Chamberlain Said* by Virginia Woodward Cloud, *Slimme Sir Marmaduke* by Henry Groff Dodge, *Two Little Men* by Malcolm Douglas, *George O'Green and Robin Hood* by Caroline Brown, *Prince Cam and the Fairies* by Sydney Reid.

TO HARCOURT, BRACE AND COMPANY for the illustrations from the following poems selected from *Rainbow in the Sky* edited by Louis Untermeyer: *Little Bo-Peep, Star-Light, The Diverting History of John Gilpin* by William Cowper, *The Owl and the Pussy-Cat* by Edward Lear; for the illustrations of poems by W. S. Gilbert selected from *The Last Pirate* by Louis Untermeyer.

TO HOUGHTON MIFFLIN COMPANY for the selection from *The Admiral's Caravan* by Charles E. Carryl.

TO CHARLES SCRIBNER'S SONS for the selection from *Little Lord Fauntleroy* by Frances Hodgson Burnett, for the selection from *The Little Princess* by Frances Hodgson Burnett, and for *The Castle of Bim* selected from *The Reformed Pirate* by Frank R. Stockton.

TO SIMON AND SCHUSTER for *The Tale of Custard the Dragon* selected from *The Bad Parents' Garden of Verse* by Ogden Nash.

TABLE OF CONTENTS

ix

TABLE OF CONTENTS

INTRODUCTION

by May Lamberton Becker

FOR ONE brief and glorious year I spent most of my waking hours within a few feet of the most fascinating bookcase in New York City. Nobody passed it quite unmoved, and scarcely anybody went by without stopping. For it contained a complete file, from the very first year to the present, of bound volumes of the old *St. Nicholas.*

The best feature of the interest thus aroused was that it was shown by old and young alike. People of my own time of life paused to look once more at a page that had introduced them to a book now classic, when it was running as a serial away back in the eighties. But when they brought their grandchildren to visit the bookcase, these up-to-date young persons would camp on the floor, surrounded by scarlet-and-gold books bound before they were born, having just as good a time and in the same way. They were not surprised to find the pictures of Reginald Birch coming in so far back in the line of volumes. He had nothing to do with dates. There must always have been Birch, they thought, and there always must be. He was one of the facts of nature to children who like pictures with their stories.

So he has been one of the facts of child nature ever since the day he opened the door and let in a little fellow in a velvet suit, his arm thrown confidingly about the neck of a great dog. That, I need not tell you, was

Little Lord Fauntleroy, and from that time to this Reginald Birch has been opening doors for children's characters and leading them into children's hearts.

Not long since, a letter came to Mr. Birch signed "A Little Boy of the Eighties." The writer had, it appears, been brought up on the *St. Nicholas* of that period. The stories that Birch had illustrated were the ones he remembered, and these pictures, he said, had been his most important experience with art. For they had meant complete fulfillment of his desires for pictures. Why should anyone else, he thought in those days, make pictures for stories when there was Birch to do them? I know how he felt. There was a rightness about those pictures. They had something we wanted and for which we had as yet no word. We did not know that it was glamour.

Now glamour has no date, no age limit. It has the same power, the same appeal, whenever it comes to us. The pictures of Reginald Birch, those of today and those of nearly sixty years ago, have the same sort of glamour that keeps the Gilbert and Sullivan operas forever young, healthy, robust and joyous. No wonder he could and did make the right pictures for Gilbert and Sullivan.

When I was little, we knew and loved our illustrators just as we loved and knew our authors—children always do, I think. We did not have to look in the corner of the picture for initials to know that this was our Abbey and that our Howard Pyle, or pick out F. S. Church, Rodgers, or Kemble, or tell the wild steeds of Remington from the trim, docked ponies of Grey-Parker. So whenever we saw a Birch, we knew it at once for our own. He somehow succeeded in making goodness not only plausible but attractive. That we did not find some heroes and heroines of the period too good to be true, was largely because we not only read about them, we saw them—as Birch meant us to see them. He not only made goodness beautiful, he wasted no beauty on badness. You could tell at a glance which were the cruel ones and which the kind. This may be one of the reasons why, in later years, he was to make the best illustrations of Dickens characters that have been made since those that Dickens supervised.

So time went on, and my generation grew up, and my daughter's generation grew up, and there was Birch meeting today's children with new pictures for new books and making them love his people in the same way and for the same reasons. It looked for a while as if he might make pictures no more: his eyes went into eclipse after he was eighty. But they came out again from under that cloud, and as his spirit had never been dimmed at all, on he went making pictures.

Then some of us thought what a good book might be made by getting together selections from some of the many books that he has illustrated— books that collectors are now beginning to treasure—to show how great a part he has had in the book world of childhood. There are "old" pictures here from "old" books, and "new" pictures from "new" ones. Children like one as they do the other. Childhood is both old and new, like spring. So is Birch. So are his drawings. This is a garland for Birch: we wove it, but he gave us the flowers.

EDITOR'S NOTE

IF ANYONE were to make a complete anthology of all the books, stories, and poems illustrated by Reginald Birch the volume would probably be at least as large as Webster's Dictionary. His first illustration published in America was made for a poem which appeared in *St. Nicholas* in 1881, when Mr. Birch was a young man of 25. His latest work to date is for a book published in 1939, in which year he is (in spirit, skill, and understanding) a young man of 83.

Through these fifty-nine years Reginald Birch has illustrated, at a safe estimate, not less than two hundred books and uncounted numbers of stories and poems appearing in magazines.

It is the purpose of this volume to collect a small part of Mr. Birch's best-known and best-loved work, and to make available again some of his drawings which are now out of print in the original form. The selection has been a difficult one to make—so many fine and enduring books for children have been "illustrated by Reginald Birch."

The selection was determined to some extent by the possibilities of reproduction of the pictures. Mr. Birch's original drawings have long been collectors' items, and are in private collections and museums here and abroad. So the pictures in this book are, with one exception, reproductions of reproductions. If, in some cases, the delicate lines and shading of this expert artist are not perfectly shown, it is because of difficulties which the engraver could not overcome, and not because of any fault in the drawing.

The one exception is the frontispiece. The original drawing of this illustration from "Little Lord Fauntleroy" is owned by Mrs. Vivian Burnett, and it is through her kindness that we are able to reproduce this illustration from the original.

We are proud to present "Reginald Birch—His Book," as a service to American children, and as a tribute to that great illustrator, Reginald Birch.

E. B. H.

March 21, 1939.

DOROTHY AND THE ADMIRAL

from The Admiral's Caravan

by Charles E. Carryl

DOROTHY AND THE ADMIRAL

DOROTHY sat on the step of the Blue Admiral Inn near the Admiral himself, on his pedestal beside the porch.

Now the Admiral was only a yard high, and was made of wood into the bargain; but he was a fine figure of a man for all that, being dressed in a very beautiful blue coat (as befitted his name) and canary-colored knee-breeches, and wearing a fore-and-aft hat rakishly perched on the back of his head. On the other hand, he had sundry stray cracks in the calves of his legs, and was badly battered about the nose; but, after all, this only gave him a certain weather-beaten appearance as if he had been around the world any number of times in all sorts of company; and for as long as Dorothy could remember he had been standing on his pedestal beside the porch, enjoying the sunshine and defying the rain, as a gallant officer should, and earnestly gazing at the opposite side of the street through a spy-glass.

Now, what the Admiral was staring at was a mystery. He might, for instance, have been looking at the wooden Highlander

3

that stood at the door of Mr. Pendle's instrument-shop, for nothing more magnificent than this particular Highlander could possibly be imagined. His clothes were of every color of the rainbow, and he had silver buckles on his shoes, and brass buttons on his coat, and he was varnished to such an extent that you could hardly look at him without winking. Then his hair and his whiskers were so red, and his legs were so pink and so fat and so life-like, that it seemed as if you could almost hear him speak; and, what was more, he had been standing for years at the door of the shop, proudly holding up a preposterous wooden watch that gave half-past three as the correct time at all hours of the day and night. In fact, it would have been no great wonder if the Admiral had stared at him to the end of his days.

Then there was Sir Walter Rosettes, a long-bodied little man in a cavalier's cloak, with a ruff about his neck and enormous rosettes on his shoes, who stood on a pedestal at old Mrs. Peevy's garden gate, offering an imitation tobacco-plant, free of charge, as it were, to anyone who would take the trouble of carrying it home.

Dorothy was watching the people hurrying by, when she suddenly noticed that the toes of the Admiral's shoes were turned sideways on his pedestal, and looking up at him she saw that he had tucked his spy-glass under his arm, and was gazing down backward at his legs with an air of great concern.

This was so startling that Dorothy almost jumped out of her shoes, and she was just turning to run back into the house when the Admiral caught sight of her, and called out excitedly, "Cracks in my legs!"—and then stared hard at her as if demanding some sort of an explanation of this extraordinary state of affairs.

Dorothy was dreadfully frightened, but she was a very polite little girl, and would have answered the town pump if it had

spoken to her; so she swallowed down a great lump that had come up into her throat, and said, as respectfully as she could, "I'm very sorry, sir. I suppose it must be because they are so very old."

"Old!" exclaimed the Admiral, making a desperate attempt to get a view of his legs through his spy-glass. "Why, they're no older than I am"; and, upon thinking it over, this seemed so very true that Dorothy felt quite ashamed of her remark and stood looking at him in a rather foolish way.

"Try again," said the Admiral, with a patronizing air.

"No," said Dorothy, gravely shaking her head, "I'm sure I don't know any other reason; only it seems rather strange, you know, that you've never even seen them before."

"If you mean my legs," said the Admiral, "of course I've seen them before—lots of times. But I've never seen 'em behind. That is," he added by way of explanation, "I've never seen 'em behind before."

"But I mean the cracks," said Dorothy, with a faint smile. You see she was beginning to feel a little acquainted with the Admiral by this time, and the conversation didn't seem to be quite so solemn as it had been when he first began talking.

7

"Then you should say 'seen 'em before *behind*,'" said the Admiral. "That's where they've always been, you know."

Dorothy didn't know exactly what reply to make to this remark; but she thought she ought to say something by way of helping along the conversation, so she began, "I suppose it's kind of—" and here she stopped to think of the word she wanted.

"Kind of what?" said the Admiral severely.

"Kind of—cripplesome, isn't it?" said Dorothy rather confusedly.

"Cripplesome?" exclaimed the Admiral. "Why, that's no word for it. It's positively decrepitoodle—" here he paused for a moment and got extremely red in the face, and then finished up with "—loodelarious," and stared hard at her again, as if inquiring what she thought of *that*.

"Goodness!" said Dorothy, drawing a long breath, "what a word!"

"Well, it *is* rather a word," said the Admiral with a very satisfied air. "You see, it means about everything that can happen to a person's legs—" but just here his remarks came abruptly to an end, for as he was strutting about on his pedestal, he suddenly slipped off the edge of it and came to the ground flat on

his back.

Dorothy gave a little scream of dismay; but the Admiral, who didn't appear to be in the least disturbed by this accident, sat up and gazed about with a complacent smile. Then, getting on his feet, he took a pipe out of his pocket, and lit it with infinite relish; and having turned up his coat-collar by way of keeping the rest of his clothes dry, he started off down the street without another word. The people going by had all disappeared in the most unaccountable manner, and Dorothy could see him

9

quite plainly as he walked along, tacking from one side of the street to the other with a strange rattling noise, and blowing little puffs of smoke into the air like a shabby little steam-tug going to sea in a storm.

Now all this was extremely exciting, and Dorothy, quite forgetting the rain, ran down the street a little way so as to keep the Admiral in sight. "It's *precisely* like a doll going traveling all by itself," she exclaimed as she ran along. "How he rattles! I suppose *that's* his little cracked legs—and goodness gracious, how he smokes!" she added, for by this time the Admiral had fired up, so to speak, as if he were bound on a long journey, and was blowing out such clouds of smoke that he presently quite shut himself out from view. The smoke smelt somewhat like burnt feathers, which, of course, was not very agreeable, but the worst of it was that when Dorothy turned to run home again she discovered that she couldn't see her way back to the porch, and she was feeling about for it with her hands stretched out, when the smoke suddenly cleared away and she found that the inn, and Mr. Pendle's shop, and Mrs. Peevy's cottage had all disappeared like a street in a pantomime, and that she was standing quite alone before a strange little stone house.

The rain had stopped, and the moon was shining through the breaking clouds, and as Dorothy looked up at the little stone house she saw that it had an archway through it with "FERRY" in large letters on the wall above it. Of course she had no idea of going by herself over a strange ferry; but she was an extremely curious little girl, as you will presently see, and so she immediately ran through the archway to see what the ferry was like and where it took people, but, to her surprise, instead of coming out at the water side, she came into a strange, old-fashioned-looking street as crooked as it could possibly be, and lined on both sides by tall houses with sharply peaked roofs looming up against the evening sky. She was just turning to go back through the archway when the door of one of the houses flew open and a little stream of water ran out upon the pavement. This was immediately followed by another and much larger flow, and the next moment the water came pouring out through the doorway in such a torrent that she had just time to scramble up on the window-ledge before the street was completely flooded.

Dorothy's first idea was that there was something wrong with the pipes, but as she peeped in curiously through the window she was astonished to see that it was raining hard inside the

house—"and dear me!" she exclaimed, "here comes all the furniture!" and, sure enough, the next moment a lot of old-fashioned furniture came floating out of the house and drifted away down the street. There was a corner cupboard full of crockery, and two spinning-wheels, and a spindle-legged table set out with a blue-and-white tea-set and some cups and saucers, and finally a carved sideboard which made two or three clumsy attempts to get through the doorway broadside on, and then took a fresh start, and came through endwise with a great flourish. All of these things made quite a little fleet, and the effect was very imposing; but by this time the water was quite up to the window-ledge, and as the sideboard was a fatherly-looking piece of furniture with plenty of room to move about in, Dorothy stepped aboard of it as it went by, and, sitting down on a little shelf that ran along the back of it, sailed away in the wake of the tea-table.

The sideboard behaved in the most absurd manner, spinning around and around in the water, and banging about among the other furniture as if it had never been at sea before, and finally bringing up against the tea-table with a crash in the stupidest way imaginable, and knocking the tea-set and all the cups and saucers into the water. Dorothy felt very ridiculous as you may suppose.

Presently the street ended at a great open space where the water spread out in every direction, like a lake. The day seemed to be breaking, and it was quite light; and as the sideboard sailed out into the open water, Dorothy caught sight of something like a fat-looking boat, floating at a little distance and slowly drifting toward her. As it came nearer it proved to be Mrs. Peevy's big umbrella upside down, with a little party of people sitting around on the edge of it with their feet against the handle, and, to Dorothy's amazement, she knew every one of them. There was the Admiral, staring about with his spy-glass, and Sir Walter Rosettes, carefully carrying his tobacco-plant as if it were a nosegay, and the Highlander, with his big watch dangling in the water over the side of the umbrella; and last, there was the little Chinese mandarin clinging convulsively to the top of the handle as if he were keeping a lookout from the masthead.

The sideboard brought up against the edge of the umbrella with a soft little bump, and the Admiral, hurriedly pointing his spy-glass at Dorothy so that the end of it almost touched her nose, exclaimed excitedly, "There she is! I can see her quite plainly," and the whole party gave an exultant shout.

"How are you getting on *now?*" inquired Sir Walter, as if he had had her under close observation for a week at least.

"I'm getting on pretty well," said Dorothy, mournfully. "I believe I'm crossing a ferry."

"So are we," said the Admiral, cheerfully. "We're a Caravan,

you know."

"A Caravan?" exclaimed Dorothy, very much surprised.

"I believe I said 'Caravan' quite distinctly," said the Admiral in an injured tone, appealing to the rest of the party; but no one said anything except the Highlander, who hastily consulted his watch and then exclaimed "Hurrah!" rather doubtfully.

"I understood what you said," explained Dorothy, "but I don't think I know exactly what you mean."

"Never mind what he means," shouted Sir Walter. *"That's* of no consequence."

"No consequence!" exclaimed the Admiral, flaring up. "Why, I mean more in a minute than you do in a week!"

"You *say* more in a minute than anybody could mean in a month," retorted Sir Walter, flourishing his tobacco-plant.

"I can talk a year without meaning *anything,"* said the Highlander, proudly; but no one took any notice of this remark, which, of course, served him right.

The Admiral stared at Sir Walter for a moment through his spy-glass, and then said very firmly, "You're a pig!" at which the Highlander again consulted his watch, and then shouted, "Two pigs!" with great enthusiasm, as if that were the time of

16

day.

"And you're another," said Sir Walter, angrily. "If it comes to that, we're all pigs."

"Dear me!" cried Dorothy, quite distressed at all this. "What makes you all quarrel so? You ought to be ashamed of yourselves."

"We're all ashamed of one another, if *that* will do any good," said the Admiral.

"And, you see, that gives each of us two persons to be ashamed of," added Sir Walter, with an air of great satisfaction.

"But that isn't what I mean at all," said Dorothy. "I mean that each one of you ought to be ashamed of *himself.*"

"Why, we're each being ashamed of by two persons already," said the Admiral, peevishly. "I should think *that* was enough to satisfy anybody."

"But that isn't the same thing," insisted Dorothy. "Each particular him ought to be ashamed of each particular self." This remark sounded very fine indeed, and Dorothy felt so pleased with herself for having made it that she went on to say, "And the truth of it is, you all argue precisely like a lot of little school-children."

Now, Dorothy herself was only about four feet high, but she said this in such a superior manner that the entire Caravan stared at her with great admiration for a moment, and then began to give a little cheer; but just at this instant the umbrella made a great plunge, as if somebody had given it a sudden push, and the whole party tumbled into the bottom of it like a lot of dolls.

"What kind of a boat do you call this?" shouted Sir Walter, as they all scrambled to their feet and clung desperately to the handle.

"It's a paragondola," said the Admiral, who had suddenly become very pale. "You see, it isn't exactly like an ordinary ship."

"I should think not!" said Sir Walter, indignantly. "I'd as lief go to sea in a toast-rack. Why don't you bring her head up to the wind?" he shouted as the paragondola took another plunge.

"I can't!" cried the Admiral, despairingly; "she hasn't got any head."

"Then put me ashore!" roared Sir Walter, furiously.

Now this was all very well for Sir Walter to say, but by this time the paragondola was racing through the water at such a rate that even the sideboard could hardly keep up with it; and the waves were tossing about in such wild confusion that it was perfectly ridiculous for anyone to talk about going ashore. In fact, it was a most exciting moment. The air was filled with flying spray, and the paragondola dashed ahead faster and faster, until at last Dorothy could no longer hear the sound of the voices, and she could just see that they were throwing the big watch overboard as if to lighten the ship. Then she caught sight of the Highlander trying to climb up the handle, and Sir Walter frantically beating him on the back with the tobacco-plant, and the next moment there was another wild plunge and the paragondola and Caravan vanished from sight.

THE TALE OF CUSTARD THE DRAGON

by Ogden Nash

Belinda lived in a little white house,
With a little black kitten and a little gray mouse,
And a little yellow dog and a little red wagon,
And a realio, trulio, little pet dragon.

Now the name of the little black kitten was Ink,
And the little gray mouse, she called her Blink,
And the little yellow dog was sharp as Mustard,
But the dragon was a coward, and she called him Custard.

Custard the dragon had big sharp teeth,
And spikes on top of him and scales underneath,
Mouth like a fireplace, chimney for a nose,
And realio, trulio daggers on his toes.

Belinda was as brave as a barrel full of bears,
And Ink and Blink chased lions down the stairs,
Mustard was as brave as a tiger in a rage,
But Custard cried for a nice safe cage.

Belinda tickled him, she tickled him unmerciful,
Ink, Blink and Mustard, they rudely called him Percival,
They all sat laughing in the little red wagon
At the realio, trulio, cowardly dragon.

Belinda giggled till she shook the house,
And Blink said Weeek!, which is giggling for a mouse,
Ink and Mustard rudely asked his age,
When Custard cried for a nice safe cage.

Suddenly, suddenly they heard a nasty sound,
And Mustard growled, and they all looked around.
Meowch! cried Ink, and Ooh! cried Belinda,
For there was a pirate, climbing in the winda.

Pistol in his left hand, pistol in his right,
And he held in his teeth a cutlass bright,
His beard was black, one leg was wood;
It was clear that the pirate meant no good.

Belinda paled, and she cried Help! Help!
But Mustard fled with a terrified yelp,
Ink trickled down to the bottom of the household,
And little mouse Blink strategically mouseholed.

But up jumped Custard, snorting like an engine,
Clashed his tail like irons in a dungeon,
With a clatter and a clank and a jangling squirm
He went at the pirate like a robin at a worm.

The pirate gaped at Belinda's dragon,
And gulped some grog from his pocket flagon,
He fired two bullets, but they didn't hit,
And Custard gobbled him, every bit.

Belinda embraced him, Mustard licked him,
No one mourned for his pirate victim.
Ink and Blink in glee did gyrate
Around the dragon that ate the pyrate.

Belinda still lives in her little white house,
With her little black kitten and her little gray mouse,
And her little yellow dog and her little red wagon,
And her realio, trulio, little pet dragon.

Belinda is as brave as a barrel full of bears,
And Ink and Blink chase lions down the stairs,
Mustard is as brave as a tiger in a rage,
But Custard keeps crying for a nice safe cage.

LORD FAUNTLEROY MEETS HIS GRANDFATHER

from LITTLE LORD FAUNTLEROY

by Frances Hodgson Burnett

LORD FAUNTLEROY MEETS HIS GRANDFATHER

IT WAS when Cedric was between seven and eight years old that the very strange thing happened which made so wonderful a change in his life. It began with earls: his grandpapa, whom he had never seen, was an earl; and his eldest uncle, if he had not been killed by a fall from his horse, would have been an earl, too, in time; and after his death, his other uncle would have been an earl, if he had not died suddenly, in Rome, of a fever. After that, his own papa, if he had lived, would have been an earl; but, since they all had died and only Cedric was left, it appeared that he was to be an earl after his grandpapa's death— and for the present he was Lord Fauntleroy.

When Mr. Havisham—who was the family lawyer of the Earl of Dorincourt, and who had been sent by him to bring Lord Fauntleroy to England—first told Mrs. Errol what he had come for, she turned very pale.

"Oh!" she said; "will he have to be taken away from me?

We love each other so much! He is all I have." And her sweet young voice trembled, and the tears rushed into her eyes. "You do not know what he has been to me!" she said.

The lawyer cleared his throat.

"I am obliged to tell you," he said, "that the Earl of Dorincourt is not—is not very friendly toward you. He is an old man, and his prejudices are very strong. He has always especially disliked America and Americans, and was very much enraged by his son's marriage. I am sorry to be the bearer of so unpleasant a communication, but he is very fixed in his determination not to see you. His plan is that Lord Fauntleroy shall be educated under his own supervision; that he shall live with him. The Earl is attached to Dorincourt Castle, and spends a great deal of time there. He is a victim to inflammatory gout, and is not fond of London. Lord Fauntleroy will, therefore, be likely to live chiefly at Dorincourt. The Earl offers you as a home Court Lodge, which is situated pleasantly, and is not very far from the castle. Lord Fauntleroy will be permitted to visit you; the only stipulation is, that you shall not visit him or enter the park gates. You see you will not be really separated from your son, and I assure you, madam, the terms are not so harsh as—as they might have been. The advantage of such surroundings and education as Lord Fauntleroy will have, I am sure you must see, will be very great."

He felt a little uneasy lest she should begin to cry or make a scene, as he knew some women would have done. It embarrassed and annoyed him to see women cry.

But she did not. She went to the window and stood with her face turned away for a few moments, and he saw she was trying to steady herself.

"I hope," she said in a rather broken voice, "that his grandfather will love Ceddie. The little boy has a very affectionate nature; and he has always been loved."

Mr. Havisham cleared his throat again. He could not quite imagine the gouty, fiery-tempered old Earl loving anyone very much; but he knew it would be to his interest to be kind, in his irritable way, to the child who was to be his heir. He knew, too, that if Ceddie were at all a credit to his name, his grandfather would be proud of him.

"Lord Fauntleroy will be comfortable, I am sure," he replied. "It was with a view to his happiness that the Earl desired that you should be near enough to see him frequently."

29

When the lawyer and Cedric were left together, Mr. Havisham wondered what he should say to his small companion. But Cedric relieved him by suddenly beginning the conversation himself.

"Do you know," he said, "I don't know what an earl is?"

"Don't you?" said Mr. Havisham.

"No," replied Ceddie. "And I think when a boy is going to be one, he ought to know. Don't you?"

"Well—yes," answered Mr. Havisham.

"Would you mind," said Ceddie respectfully—"would you mind 'splaining it to me?" (Sometimes when he used his long words he did not pronounce them quite correctly.)

"There is an advantage in being an earl, sometimes," said Mr. Havisham slowly, and he fixed his shrewd eyes on the little boy with a rather curious expression. "Some earls have a great deal of money."

He was curious because he wondered if his young friend knew what the power of money was.

"That's a good thing to have," said Ceddie innocently. "I wish I had a great deal of money."

"Do you?" said Mr. Havisham. "And why?"

30

"Well," explained Cedric, "there are so many things a person can do with money. You see, there's the apple-woman. If I were very rich I should buy her a little tent to put her stall in, and a

31

little stove, and then I should give her a dollar every morning it rained, so that she could afford to stay at home. And then Dick—"

"Who is Dick?" asked Mr. Havisham.

"Dick is a boot-black," said his young lordship, quite warming up in his interest in plans so exciting.

"And what would you like to do for him?" inquired the lawyer, rubbing his chin and smiling a queer smile.

"Well," said Lord Fauntleroy, settling himself in his chair with a business air, "I'd buy Jake out."

"And who is Jake?" Mr. Havisham asked.

"He's Dick's partner, and he is the worst partner a fellow could have! He cheats, and that makes Dick mad."

In truth Mr. Havisham was beginning to be greatly interested; but perhaps not quite so much in Dick and the apple-woman as in this kind little lordling, whose curly head was so busy, under its yellow thatch, with good-natured plans for his friends, and who seemed somehow to have forgotten himself altogether.

.   .   .   .

It was late in the afternoon when the carriage containing little Lord Fauntleroy and Mr. Havisham drove up the long avenue which led to the castle. The Earl had given orders that his grandson should arrive in time to dine with him; and for some reason best known to himself, he had also ordered that the child should be sent alone into the room in which he intended to receive him.

The carriage rolled on and on between the great, beautiful trees which grew on each side of the avenue and stretched their broad, swaying branches in an arch across it. Cedric had never seen such trees—they were so grand and stately, and their branches grew so low down on their huge trunks. He liked the big, broad-branched trees, with the late afternoon sunlight striking golden lances through them. He liked the perfect stillness which rested on everything. He felt a great, strange pleasure in the beauty of which he caught glimpses under and between the sweeping boughs—the great, beautiful spaces of the park, with still other trees standing sometimes stately and alone, and sometimes in groups. Now and then they passed places where tall ferns grew in masses, and again and again the ground was azure with the bluebells swaying in the soft breeze. Several times he started up with a laugh of delight as a rabbit leaped up from under the greenery and scudded away with a twinkle of short white tail behind it. Once a covey of partridges rose with a sudden whir and flew away, and then he shouted and clapped his hands.

"It's a beautiful place, isn't it?" he said to Mr. Havisham. "I never saw such a beautiful place. It's prettier even than Central Park."

He was rather puzzled by the length of time they were on their way.

"How far is it," he said, at length, "from the gate to the front door?"

"It is between three and four miles," answered the lawyer.

"That's a long way for a person to live from his gate," remarked his lordship.

Every few minutes he saw something new to wonder at and admire. When he caught sight of the deer, some couched in the grass, some standing with their pretty antlered heads turned with a half-startled air toward the avenue as the carriage wheels disturbed them, he was enchanted.

"Has there been a circus?" he cried; "or do they live here always? Whose are they?"

"They live here," Mr. Havisham told him. "They belong to the Earl, your grandfather."

It was not long after this that they saw the castle. It rose up before them stately and beautiful and gray, the last rays of the sun casting dazzling lights on its many windows. It had turrets and battlements and towers; a great deal of ivy grew upon its walls; all the broad, open space about it was laid out in terraces and lawns and beds of brilliant flowers.

"It's the most beautiful place I ever saw!" said Cedric, his round face flushing with pleasure. "It reminds anyone of a king's palace. I saw a picture of one once in a fairy-book."

A few minutes later, the very tall footman in livery, who had escorted Cedric to the library door, opened it and announced: "Lord Fauntleroy, my lord," in quite a majestic tone. If he were only a footman, he felt it was rather a grand occasion when the heir came home to his own land and possessions, and was ushered into the presence of the old Earl, whose place and title he was to take.

Cedric crossed the threshold into the room. It was a very large and splendid room, with massive carven furniture in it, and shelves upon shelves of books; the furniture was so dark, and the draperies so heavy, the diamond-paned windows were so deep, and it seemed such a distance from one end of it to the other, that, since the sun had gone down, the effect of it all was rather gloomy. For a moment Cedric thought there was nobody in the room, but soon he saw that by the fire burning on the wide hearth there was a large easy-chair and that in that chair someone was sitting—someone who did not at first turn to look at him.

But he had attracted attention in one quarter at least. On the floor, by the arm-chair, lay a dog, a huge tawny mastiff, with body and limbs almost as big as a lion's; and this great creature rose majestically and slowly, and marched toward the little fellow with a heavy step.

Then the person in the chair spoke. "Dougal," he called, "come back, sir."

But there was no more fear in little Lord Fauntleroy's heart than there was unkindness—he had been a brave little fellow all his life. He put his hand on the big dog's collar in the most natural way in the world, and they strayed forward together, Dougal sniffing as he went.

And then the Earl looked up. What Cedric saw was a large old man with shaggy white hair and eyebrows, and a nose like an eagle's beak between his deep, fierce eyes. What the Earl saw was a graceful, childish figure in a black velvet suit, with a lace

collar, and with love-locks waving about the handsome, manly little face, whose eyes met his with a look of innocent good-fellowship. If the castle was like the palace in a fairy story, it must be owned that little Lord Fauntleroy was himself rather like a small copy of the fairy prince, though he was not at all aware of the fact, and perhaps was rather a sturdy young model of a fairy. But there was a sudden glow of triumph and exultation in the fiery old Earl's heart as he saw what a strong, beautiful boy this grandson was, and how unhesitatingly he looked up as he stood with his hand on the big dog's neck. It pleased the grim old nobleman that the child should show no shyness or fear, either of the dog or of himself.

Cedric came quite close to him.

"Are you the Earl?" he said. "I'm your grandson, you know, that Mr. Havisham brought. I'm Lord Fauntleroy."

He held out his hand because he thought it must be the polite and proper thing to do even with earls. "I hope you are very well," he continued, with the utmost friendliness. "I'm very glad to see you."

The Earl shook hands with him, with a curious gleam in his eyes; just at first, he was so astonished that he scarcely knew what to say. He stared at the picturesque little apparition from under his shaggy brows, and took it all in from head to foot. "Glad to see me, are you?" he said.

"Yes," answered Lord Fauntleroy, "very."

There was a chair near him, and he sat down on it; it was a high-backed, rather tall chair, and his feet did not touch the floor when he had settled himself in it, but he seemed to be quite comfortable as he sat there, and regarded his august relative intently but modestly.

"I've kept wondering what you would look like," he remarked. "I used to lie in my berth in the ship and wonder if you would be anything like my father."

"Am I?" asked the Earl.

"Well," Cedric replied, "I was very young when he died, and I may not remember exactly how he looked, but I don't think you are like him."

"You are disappointed, I suppose?" suggested his grandfather.

"Oh, no," responded Cedric politely. "Of course you would like anyone to look like your father; but of course you would enjoy the way your grandfather looked, even if he wasn't like your father. You know how it is yourself about admiring your relations."

The Earl leaned back in his chair and stared. He could not be said to know how it was about admiring his relations. He had employed most of his noble leisure in quarreling violently with them, in turning them out of his house, and applying abusive epithets to them; and they all hated him cordially.

"Any boy would love his grandfather," continued Lord Fauntleroy, "especially one that had been as kind to him as you have been."

"Oh!" he said, "I have been kind to you, have I?"

"Yes," answered Lord Fauntleroy brightly; "I'm ever so much obliged to you about Bridget, and the apple-woman, and Dick."

"Bridget!" exclaimed the Earl. "Dick! The apple-woman!"

"Yes!" explained Cedric; "the ones you gave me all that money for—the money you told Mr. Havisham to give me if I wanted it."

"Ha!" ejaculated his lordship. "That's it, is it? The money you were to spend as you liked. What did you buy with it? I should like to hear something about that."

He drew his shaggy eyebrows together and looked at the child sharply. He was secretly curious to know in what way the lad had indulged himself.

"Oh!" said Lord Fauntleroy, "perhaps you didn't know about Dick and the apple-woman and Bridget. I forgot you lived such a long way off from them. They were particular friends of mine. And you see Michael had the fever—"

"Who's Michael?" asked the Earl.

"Michael is Bridget's husband, and they were in great trouble. When a man is sick and can't work and has twelve children, you know how it is. And Michael has always been a sober man. And Bridget used to come to our house and cry. And the evening Mr. Havisham was there, she was in the kitchen crying, because they had almost nothing to eat and couldn't pay the rent; and I went in to see her, and Mr. Havisham sent for me and he said you had given him some money for me. And I ran as fast as I could into the kitchen and gave it to Bridget; and that made it all right; and Bridget could scarcely believe her eyes. That's why I'm so obliged to you."

"Oh!" said the Earl in his deep voice, "that was one of the things you did for yourself, was it? What else?"

Dougal had been sitting by the tall chair; the great dog had taken its place there when Cedric sat down. Several times it had

41

turned and looked up at the boy as if interested in the conversation. Dougal was a solemn dog, who seemed to feel altogether too big to take life's responsibilities lightly. The old Earl, who knew the dog well, had watched it with secret interest. Dougal was not a dog whose habit was to make acquaintances rashly, and the Earl wondered somewhat to see how quietly the brute sat under the touch of the childish hand. And, just at this moment, the big dog gave little Lord Fauntleroy one more look of dignified scrutiny, and deliberately laid its huge, lion-like head on the boy's velvet knee.

The small hand went on stroking this new friend as Cedric answered:

"Well, there was Dick," he said. "He's a professional boot-black."

"And he's one of your acquaintances, is he?" said the Earl.

"He is an old friend of mine," replied his grandson.

The sensations of the Right Honorable the Earl of Dorincourt could scarcely be described. He was not an old nobleman who was very easily bewildered, because he had seen a great deal of the world; but here was something he found so novel that it almost took his lordly breath away, and caused him some singular emotions. He had never cared for children; he had been so occupied with his own pleasures that he had never had time to care for them. He had been so selfish himself that he had missed the pleasure of seeing unselfishness in others, and he had not known how tender and faithful and affectionate a kind-hearted little child can be, and how innocent and unconscious are its simple, generous impulses. It had never once occurred to him that he should like his grandson; he had sent for the little Cedric because his pride impelled him to do so. If the boy was to take his place in the future, he did not wish his name to be made ridiculous by descending to an uneducated boor. When the footman had announced Lord Fauntleroy, he had almost dreaded to look at the boy lest he should find him all that he had feared. It was because of this feeling that he had ordered that the child should be sent to him alone. His pride could not endure that others should see his disappointment if he was to be disappointed. His proud, stubborn old heart therefore had leaped within him when the boy came forward with his graceful, easy carriage, his fearless hand on the big dog's neck. Even in the moments when he had hoped the most, the Earl had never hoped that his grandson would look like that. The Earl's stern composure was quite shaken by this startling surprise.

And then their talk began; and he was still more curiously moved, and more and more puzzled. In the first place, he was so used to seeing people rather afraid and embarrassed before him, that he had expected nothing else but that his grandson would be timid or shy. But Cedric was no more afraid of the Earl than he had been of Dougal. He was not bold; he was only innocently friendly, and he was not conscious that there could be any reason why he should be awkward or afraid.

When dinner was announced, Cedric left his chair and went to his noble kinsman. He looked down at his gouty foot.

"Would you like me to help you?" he said politely. "You could lean on me, you know."

The big footman almost periled his reputation and his situation by smiling. He was an aristocratic footman who had always lived in the best of noble families, and had never smiled; indeed, he would have felt himself a disgraced and vulgar footman if he had allowed himself to be led by any circumstance whatever into such an indiscretion as a smile. But he had a very narrow escape. He only just saved himself by staring straight over the Earl's head at a very ugly picture.

The Earl looked his valiant young relative over from head to foot.

"Do you think you could do it?" he asked gruffly.

"I *think* I could," said Cedric. "I'm strong. I'm seven, you know. You could lean on your stick on one side, and on me on the other. Dick says I've a good deal of muscle for a boy that's only seven."

He shut his hand and moved it upward to his shoulder, so that the Earl might see the muscle Dick had kindly approved of, and his face was so grave and earnest that the footman found it necessary to look very hard indeed at the ugly picture.

"Well," said the Earl, "you may try."

Cedric gave him his stick and began to assist him to rise. Usually, the footman did this, and was violently sworn at when his lordship had an extra twinge of gout. The Earl was not a very polite person as a rule, and many a time the huge footmen about him quaked inside their imposing liveries.

But this evening he did not swear, though his gouty foot gave him more twinges than one. He chose to try an experiment. He got up slowly and put his hand on the small shoulder presented to him with so much courage. Little Lord Fauntleroy made a careful step forward, looking down at the gouty foot.

"Just lean on me," he said, with encouraging good cheer. "I'll walk very slowly."

If the Earl had been supported by the footman he would have rested less on his stick and more on his assistant's arm. And yet it was part of his experiment to let his grandson feel his burden as no light weight. It was quite a heavy weight indeed, and after a few steps his young lordship's face grew quite hot, and his heart beat rather fast, but he braced himself sturdily, remembering his muscle and Dick's approval of it.

"Don't be afraid of leaning on me," he panted. "I'm all right —if—if it isn't a very long way."

It was not really very far to the dining-room, but it seemed rather a long way to Cedric, before they reached the chair at the head of the table. The hand on his shoulder seemed to grow heavier at every step, and his face grew redder and hotter, and his breath shorter, but he never thought of giving up; he stiffened his childish muscles, held his head erect, and encouraged the Earl as he limped along.

"Does your foot hurt you very much when you stand on it?" he asked. "Did you ever put it in hot water and mustard? Arnica

is a very nice thing, they tell me."

The big dog walked slowly beside them, and the big footman followed; several times he looked very queer as he watched the little figure making the very most of all its strength, and bearing its burden with such good-will. The Earl, too, looked rather queer, once, as he glanced sidewise down at the flushed little face. When they entered the room where they were to dine, Cedric saw it was a very large and imposing one, and that the footman who stood behind the chair at the head of the table stared very hard as they came in.

But they reached the chair at last. The hand was removed from his shoulder, and the Earl was fairly seated.

Cedric took out his handkerchief and wiped his forehead.

"It's a warm night, isn't it?" he said. "Perhaps you need a fire because of your foot, but it seems just a little warm to me."

His delicate consideration for his noble relative's feelings was such that he did not wish to seem to intimate that any of his surroundings were unnecessary.

"You have been doing some rather hard work," said the Earl.

"Oh, no!" said Lord Fauntleroy, "it wasn't exactly hard, but I got a little warm. A person will get warm in summer time."

And he rubbed his damp curls rather vigorously with the handkerchief. His own chair was placed at the other end of the table, opposite his grandfather's. It was a chair with arms, and intended for a much larger individual than himself; indeed, everything he had seen so far—the great rooms, with their high ceilings, the massive furniture, the big footman, the big dog, the Earl himself—were all of proportions calculated to make this little lad feel that he was very small indeed. But that did not trouble him; he had never thought himself very large or important, and he was quite willing to accommodate himself even to circumstances which rather overpowered him.

Cedric finished his dinner first, and then leaned back in his chair and took a survey of the room.

"You must be very proud of your house," he said, "it's such a beautiful house. I never saw anything so beautiful; but, of course, as I'm only seven, I haven't seen much."

"And you think I must be proud of it, do you?" said the Earl.

"I should think anyone would be proud of it," replied Lord Fauntleroy. "I should be proud of it if it were my house. Everything about it is beautiful. And the park, and those trees—how beautiful they are, and how the leaves rustle!"

Then he paused an instant and looked across the table rather wistfully.

"It's a very big house for just two people to live in, isn't it?" he said.

"It is quite large enough for two," answered the Earl. "Do you find it too large?"

His little lordship hesitated a moment.

"I was only thinking," he said, "that if two people lived in it who were not very good companions, they might feel lonely sometimes."

"Do you think I shall make a good companion?" inquired the Earl.

"Yes," replied Cedric, "I think you will. Mr. Hobbs and I were great friends. He was the best friend I had except Dearest."

The Earl made a quick movement of his bushy eyebrows.

"Who is Dearest?"

"She is my mother," said Lord Fauntleroy, in a rather low, quiet little voice.

Perhaps he was a trifle tired, as his bed-time was nearing, and perhaps after the excitement of the last few days it was natural he should be tired, so perhaps, too, the feeling of weariness brought to him a vague sense of loneliness in the remembrance that tonight he was not to sleep at home, watched over by the loving eyes of that "best friend" of his. They had always been "best friends," this boy and his young mother. He could not help thinking of her, and the more he thought of her the less was he inclined to talk, and by the time the dinner was at an end the Earl saw that there was a faint shadow on his face. But Cedric bore himself with excellent courage, and when they went back to the library, though the tall footman walked on one side of his master, the Earl's hand rested on his grandson's shoulder, though not so heavily as before.

When the footman left them alone, Cedric put his hands in his small pockets, and began to walk to and fro. His eyes were very bright, and his lips were pressed together, but he kept his head up and walked firmly. Dougal moved lazily and looked at him, and then stood up. He walked over to the child, and began to follow him uneasily. Fauntleroy drew one hand from his pocket and laid it on the dog's head.

"He's a very nice dog," he said. "He's my friend. He knows how I feel."

"How do you feel?" asked the Earl.

It disturbed him to see the struggle the little fellow was having with his first feeling of homesickness, but it pleased him to see that he was making so brave an effort to bear it well. He liked this childish courage.

"Come here," he said.

Fauntleroy went to him.

"I never was away from my own house before," said the boy, with a troubled look in his brown eyes. "It makes a person feel a strange feeling when he has to stay all night in another person's castle instead of in his own house. But Dearest is not very far away from me. She told me to remember that."

He sat very quiet after this, and looked at the fire for some time.

The Earl did not speak again. He leaned back in his chair and watched him. A great many strange new thoughts passed through the old nobleman's mind. Dougal had stretched himself out and gone to sleep with his head on his huge paws. There was a long silence.

In about half an hour's time Mr. Havisham was ushered in. The great room was very still when he entered. The Earl was still leaning back in his chair. He moved as Mr. Havisham approached, and held up his hand in a gesture of warning—it seemed as if he had scarcely intended to make the gesture—as if it were almost involuntary. Dougal was still asleep, and close beside the great dog, sleeping also, with his curly head upon his arm, lay little Lord Fauntleroy.

SONG OF THE LORD CHANCELLOR

from IOLANTHE

by W. S. Gilbert

The Law is the true embodiment
Of everything that's excellent.
It has no kind of fault or flaw,
And I, my Lords, embody the Law.
The constitutional guardian I
Of pretty young Wards in Chancery,
All very agreeable girls—and none
Are over the age of twenty-one.
A pleasant occupation for
A rather susceptible Chancellor!

But though the compliment implied
Inflates me with legitimate pride,
It nevertheless can't be denied
That it has its inconvenient side.
For I'm not so old, and not so plain,
And I'm quite prepared to marry again,
But there'd be the deuce to pay in the Lords
If I fell in love with one of my Wards!
 Which rather tries my temper, for
 I'm *such* a susceptible Chancellor!

And everyone who'd marry a Ward
Must come to me for my accord,
And in my court I sit all day,
Giving agreeable girls away,
With one for him—and one for he—
And one for you—and one for ye—
And one for thou—and one for thee—
But never, oh, never a one for me!
 Which is exasperating for
 A highly susceptible Chancellor!

THE SCRIBE OF DURLEY

by Virginia Woodward Cloud

Said the dauntless Scribe of Durley, "I shall hie me forth to see

The midnight raiders who molest my favorite plum-tree.

Yestreen I counted thirty plums a-ripening in all;

This evening only twenty-nine are hanging on the wall!

"I'll fright the bold marauders forever from the scene,
For tales of blood and daring my daily food have been.
My grandsire was a warrior who fought by sea and land:
I'll sally out upon the field, his weapons in my hand!"

So that dauntless Scribe of Durley, when the night was dark and
   still,
And the trees were black and spectral, and the moon hung o'er
   the hill,
His project hazardous he hid from his maiden daughters three,
But made him ready to protect his favorite plum-tree.

"I'll don my grandsire's armor," quoth he unto himself;
"And with his shield and helmet, his long sword from the shelf,
I'll impress these poor marauders, when I conquer face to face,
That they're honored in encountering a very ancient race!"

It was a black and gloomy way, and stealthily stole he—
This dauntless Scribe of Durley—toward his favorite plum-tree;
And the gruesome armor's rusty greaves they rattled as he trod,
And the dinted helmet swayed and bent with spectral beck and
   nod.

He crawled within the shadows dark, and clambered up the wall,
When lo! upon the further side uprose a figure tall—
A fearful, ghostly figure, with hairy visage black!
And the dauntless Scribe of Durley from off the wall fell back.

Forgot was grandsire's valor, as straightway to the ground
He rolled with creak and jangle, with weird and awful sound.
Up through that gloomy garden-close the Scribe of Durley fled;
Dropped armor, shield and long sword, and the helmet from his
    head.

And lo! upon his threshold, trembling and panting, he—
The dauntless Scribe of Durley—met his pretty daughters three.
One had a lighted candle, and one the snuffers bore,
And one a gruesome cobweb-brush held valiantly before.

"Oh, father, you are come too late!" cried One and Two and
    Three;
"For armèd men this night besieged your favorite plum-tree!

We heard them stealing stealthily, and followed, one and all,
With our long broom made ready to sweep them from the wall!

And when their leader rose on high with rattling, warlike sound,
We lifted yonder cobweb-broom and felled him to the ground!
And not a plum molested is, upon your favorite tree,
For twenty-nine a-ripening are, and one we ate for tea!"

Then the dauntless Scribe of Durley, oh, ne'er a word said he
About the bold old ancestor who fought by land and sea.
Nay, he patted condescendingly each pretty daughter's head,
And with candle—and with dignity—betook himself to bed.

A YARN OF SAILOR BEN'S
by Tudor Jenks

A YARN OF SAILOR BEN'S

IN THE blue shadow of the Life-Saving Station sat Sailor Ben painting a toy boat. He ran a red stripe around the hull.

"That brightens her a bit," remarked Sailor Ben. "I hopes the little lad will like her. Anyhow, she's wuth the half-dollar —every cent."

"That's gay!" said a small boy in a sailor-suit, who just then came down the board walk from the hotel. "She'll scoot along, won't she?"

"Sure-ly," answered Sailor Ben, solemnly; "she can't help her-self. She's the model image of the 'Speedy Susan,' and that was the slickest little brig I ever see point forefoot toward blue water."

"Was she wrecked?" asked the boy.

"O' course she were," answered the old sailor. "She were bound to be—always sailing smack up agin all the coral reefs she could find. She was tradin' in the South Pacific, and she had a fancy for coral reefs. She couldn't keep clear of 'em. We hauled her off a matter of a dozen times, but it wasn't no sort o' use. She'd make up her mind to be wrecked—and wrecked she were, on the Tapioca Islands."

"Tapioca?" the boy asked, smiling doubtfully.

"Tapioca is what we called 'em. It may 'a' been Tappy-appy-oca or Tapioca-oca, but it don't signify. That ain't the point. The point is here: How did the Cook and the Bo's'n—that was me —get away from the cannibal savages?" asked Sailor Ben, very impressively. "You might read your 'Swiss Family Crusoe' forty times without comin' within forty fathom of guessin' that little riddle."

"Tell me about it," said the boy eagerly.

"Are you sure you can lie by while I'm tellin' it? I don't like to have you signaled for just as I get all sail drawin'.'"

"I can wait for half an hour," the boy answered. "They've all gone in bathing."

"Then put a stopper on that little chatter-box, open both your hearin'-ports, and—don't believe all an old sailor tells you when he's spinnin' yarns to a little landlubber," said Sailor Ben, with a good-natured chuckle. "Here's the way it goes."

.   .   .   .

As I remarked in the start, the "Speedy Susan" wrecked herself

off the Tappy-appy-oca Islands in the South Pacific. I was a green youngster then, but with the makin's of a sailor about me. After the brig bumped coral and filled, she thought she'd make a call on Mr. Davy Jones. Not havin' been invited, I made up my mind to stay above water as long as I could.

"Come," says I to the Cook, "you and me ain't captains o' this ungrateful craft. Our betters may go down in glory with the ship, but bo's'ns and cooks can't be spared like officers, and swimmin' ashore is all we're good for."

The Cook was a level-headed kind of a darky—he made the best plum-duff I ever see—and he says: "All right, sah." So over we went like a couple o' flying-fish, and come up like two tortoises. But it was a powerful stretch to swim, bein' a matter o' forty mile or so; and I mistrust whether we mightn't 'a' joined Mr. D. Jones's little party down below if it hadn't been for the Bo's'n (me). When I heard Snowball (the Cook, you mind) puffing grampus-fashion, I says to him, says I:

"Snowball, you sunburnt sea-cook, float on your back and I'll tow you a bit." So he did, and I grappled his wool and towed him as easy as if he were the Lord Mayor o' London in his kerridge. When I begin to puff like a steam-tug, Snowball played

70

horse for me while I lay baskin' like a lazy whale o' Sunday. So we went—Bo's'n tugging Cook, and Cook repayin' the compliment till we got in soundin's.

"I'm not a-goin' to describe the Tappy-appy Islands. You've got your Jography, and you can read about 'em any time. The only thing that's pecooliar about the islands you'll see as I get along with my facts.

We come ashore in good shape, water-logged, but sound in every timber, and chipper as marines in a ca'm. We had nothin' but our togs to look after, and we set there makin' observations on the weather and the good qualities of our late shipmates, till we had drained off some. Then we begun to talk of explorin' a bit.

We hadn't fixed on a plan when somethin' happened that knocked our plans into a cocked hat. Up came a lot of natives rigged out in feathers and things, jabberin' seventeen to the dozen, and maybe more. They surrounded us, and we hauled down our flags without firin' a gun—which we hadn't any. They decorated us with grass-rope bracelets, tied us into two shipshape bits o' cargo, shouldered us, and set sail inland, singin' songs o' triump'.

"Cook," says I, "we're a-goin' int' the interior."

"I'm afeard we be," he pipes up sorrowful enough, thinkin' I meant they was cannibals.

"Avast!" says I. "Men don't sing when they're hungry."

And I was right. When they got us up to their town, they cast us loose, and gave us free board and fair lodgin's, considerin' —for you wouldn't be wantin' electric-bells and bills-o'-fare in such outlandish regions.

Skippin' the months when we was just gettin' acquainted with their ways, I'll get on to the adventure part. I'll say no more than that we lived in clover, till Cook he begun to be homesick. I didn't mind it myself.

"Cook," says I, "it's a kind of copper-colored vacation when you look at it right—reg'lar rations and nothin' to do."

"It ain't like New Bedford," was all he'd say; and the same I couldn't deny.

But I'd picked up their lingo till I could converse fair and free like a genteel Tappy-appyocan, passin' the time o' day with the best of 'em. But the Cook was diff'rent; he had a wife and little kids at home, and there wasn't any way of hearin' from them. He had been the darkest darky on the islands, but he faded to the shade of a chaplain's every-day coat at the end of a long cruise.

I felt sorry for him.

So one day, though I had an invitation to play *tenny-tenny hop-hop*—which, queerly enough, wasn't unlike tennis and hop-scotch mixed up together—I politely begged off, and piloted the Cook down to the "sad sea waves" (as I once heard a sweet-singin' young woman remark).

"Cooky," says I, "you are most shockin' pale, and unstiddy upon your pins. Are you land-sick?"

"Ter tell de trufe, sah," says he, "I am wantin' powerful to git back ter ole New Bedford; and I don't see dat dese oncivilized colored pussons are goin' ter let us go."

"Well, cheer up," says I; "for I've calculated a course that oughter fetch us clear."

I made out a chart of my idee, and the black Cook he "yah-yahed" till he reminded me of a high-striking hyena what I once seen in a circus. But it was no wonder.

The way of it was this: the chief of the Tappy-appyocans was goin' to give a big blow-out—a regular plum-duff and soft-Tommy spread: plenty o' the best, and charge it to the steward; and he set great store by makin' a show for reasons that I happened to know. That's what made me think of my plan, and

74

that's why the Cook grinned.

So back we went to find the chief—Tiffin, I called him—and I hailed him till he came out from his hut where he'd been palaverin' with his chief cook.

"Tiffin," says I, "great Chief of the Tappy-appies" (for these benighted heathen like titles, and has no idee of the glorious off-hand ways of a republic like ours), "you're goin' to give a noble eatin'-match?"

"True, Moonface," says he; for that's the name I went by, though I was more like a beet in the face than like the moon.

"I s'pose you want things to go off in tip-top style?" I went on as easy as you please.

"You know well, Moonface," says he, his complexion gettin' a shade darker, "that my brother, the chief of the Succotash Islands" (there's where my memory's not what it should be—I don't rightly remember the Jography name) "is to dine with me, and he has far and away the champion cook o' these parts. Three wars have we fit over that there cook."

"I don't recall mentionin' the fact previously," I remarks, "but Snowball here—he's the boss medicine-man over a galley-stove that I ever saw" (that's the sense of what I said)—"in fact, he's

75

the chief-cook and first-chop bottle-washer of your pale brothers!"

"Well, well!" says the chief, after a spell, and lookin' at Snow-ball with int'rest. "You do surprise me."

"Yes, sirree!" I went on, slapping the cook on the shoulder, and 'most keelin' him over. "But to tell you the plain facts o' the case, his heart pants for the land of his people." (These savages delight in poetry talk, and I had picked it up along with their

76

lingo.) "His neck is stretched with gazin' towards the land o' the free and the home o' the brave!"

O' course *he* never knew the words was a quotation from a popular ballad, and it moved him—it came so sudden. Still he didn't give right in. He saw where I was a-steerin', but didn't choose to let on. So at last I purtended to be a little hurt an' huffy:

"All correct," I says; "if Cook and me can't go home to my country 'tis of thee, you sha'n't serve up to your dusky friend the great food of the pale brothers!" and I whistled "Yankee Doodle" slow and solemn, like a hymn tune.

That was too much for him.

"If I might have plenty of this great puddin', I maybe would let you go," he says, after a long think. "But I'd like to taste a sample fust."

"It's a go!" I says, takin' him up right off.

Now, the queer point about these islands was the fact that a humpin' big mount'in rose right in the middle o' the largest one. It was a played-out volcano, and the top of its peak was covered with real snow. That's what put the notion into my mind first off.

That afternoon me and the cook climbed that peak and fetched

down baskets full of snow and chunks of ice. Then we cut two
sections of bamboo—one as big as a water-butt and the other not
quite so big. There was plenty of salt alongshore, and we toted
some to the grove.

The cook he loaded the littler bamboo nearly to the muzzle
with goat's milk, and dumped in a couple o' dozen o' turtle-eggs,
and sweetened the mess to taste with sugar-cane juice—and then
we fixed a long bamboo pole to the small cask inside, and round

I went as if it was a capstan-bar. Round and *round,* round and *round!* And round, some more—till my back was breakin' with it.

But it froze stiff; and when we fished it out, it was a kind of oncivilized ice-cream. The cook he tasted it, in the way o' duty; but he looked worser than when he was homesickest.

"No, thanky," says I, when he offered me a dose; "but don't look blue, Cooky. It'll go down with these heathens—you see if it don't."

It did. You orter 've seen the chief smile when he got some— why, his grin lit up the landscape.

"Moonface Medicine-man," says he, as he scraped the sides o' the bamboo bowl we gave him, "your chill-puddin' is the finest thing I ever saw! Prepare a hundred calabashes for the Chief of the Succotash Islands, and you shall go free. I will make him knock his head to the dust!"

"It's a bargain, great Chief!" says I, and he marched back to his hut as proud as a new commodore on Sunday. You see, we were careful to give the chief a safe dose, and we fired the rest into the bushes.

Well, just before the great day we set a gang of natives to totin' down snow and ice, cuttin' bamboo for freezers, crushin' sugar-cane, and gatherin' turtle-eggs. We made enough o' the awful stuff to sink an Indiaman, and left it packed in snow in a cool place in the woods.

The day of the grand barbecue came.

First our chief he put on a poor face, and trotted out regular old played-out native dishes—*bong-bong,* and *maboo-taboo,* fried *cush-cush*—common dishes such as a third-rate chief might have 'most any day. I see the other chief's lip curlin' up till it 'most hid his snub-nose—with scorn, and with pride in his own cook. But our chief was just a-leadin' old Succotash on—foolin' him, you see.

Then come dessert. Our chief he remarks, careless and easy:

"I have a new dish, royal brother, if you will try it?"

"Don't care if I do," says the other, as if not carin' particular about it.

Our chief he whacked a gong, and in came a string of mahogany slaves proudly supportin' fancy calabashes loaded with that outlandish ice-cream.

"What, may I ask, is this?" asks the royal guest, a trifle oneasy, mistrustin' the other potentater was a-savin' his trumps for the last trick.

"Moonface chill-puddin'!" says our chief, impressive and grand.

It was set out, and at the word o' command every noble guest dipped into his calabash. Words o' mine can't depict that scene. I'd have to talk French to do it. It was like the finish of a tub-race. When I saw them all a-eatin' fast when they could, and a-tryin' to warm their froze noses when they couldn't, I nudged Snowball on the sly.

"Cook," I whispers, "we'll start now, I guess. Those fellers don't mean to stop as long as they can lift a spoon—and I'm afraid they'll overdo this thing. If we waits till dyspepsy sets in, we'll never see Hail Columbia any more."

He saw the sense o' my remark, and we got out and scooted. I hoped they wouldn't eat more than human natur' would stand —but when I thought o' that mixture, my heart kind of rose in my throat.

We didn't get away too early. Our dugout had a start, but soon we made out a war-canoe putting after us.

"Can they overhaul us?" I asks the Cook.

"No, sah!" he says, positive-like, and with a grin. "You jest wait till that pison get a fair chance!"

And by the time they got within hailin' distance, most o' the paddlers had keeled over, one by one, into the hold o' their canoe. Then she came to a dead halt. It was just in time, too, for the chief he stood up near the idol they had for a bow, waving his club, and his voice came faint over the water:

"If I catch you, you have to eat your own chill-puddin'! All my people are tumbled over with bad magic!"

"Adoo, Chief!" I sings out. "We was afraid you'd eat too much!"

He bowled a war-club at us, but he wasn't feelin' strong, and then he keeled over; and that was the last of the Tappy-appy-ocas.

.   .   .   .

"Now, here's your boat," said Sailor Ben, as he finished the story. "Let her get good and dry, or you'll be gettin' your clothes mussed up with it."

"Thank you ever so much for the boat, and for the story, too," said the little boy, as he took the new boat daintily by the mast-head.

"I hope," said Sailor Ben, looking after his little friend, and picking up his paint and brushes, "that the little landlubber didn't believe all that nonsense. He seemed rather serious and solemn over it."

LITTLE BO-PEEP

Little Bo-Peep has lost her sheep
   And can't tell where to find them;
Leave them alone, and they'll come home,
   Wagging their tails behind them.

Little Bo-Peep fell fast asleep,
　　And dreamt she heard them bleating;
But when she awoke, she found it a joke,
　　For they were still a-fleeting.

Then up she took her little crook,
  Determined for to find them;
She found them indeed; but it made her heart bleed,
  For they'd left all their tails behind them.

It happened one day, as Bo-Peep did stray
  Under a meadow hard by,
There she espied their tails side by side,
  All hung on a tree to dry.

A DAY WITH BABY

by Malcolm Douglas

The baby I'm acquainted with
    Knows naught of battle's harms,
Although he's of the infantry,
    And often up in arms.

He puts his grandpa's glasses on,
  Then imitates his frown,
And reads the paper backward, while
  He holds it upside down.

Sometimes he cries, and oh, so hard,
  I think he understood
The good old doctor when he said
  That it would do him good.

With kitty oft upon the rug
He has a wrestling match,
And kitty, it may be, will win
By just the merest scratch.

He croons a little song that sounds
  Like "Gum, oh, gum with me!"
And, as he is a minor, he
  Selects a minor key.

Each day nurse wheels him to the park,
  So, in his carriage there,
A little son and heir may find
  A little sun and air.

As in his crib he dozes off,
  With such a funny snore,
We wish he'd sleep till eight, instead
  Of waking up at four.

THE MAY-DAY PLAY
from MASTER SKYLARK

by John Bennett

ALL COVENTRY was thronged with people come to see the May-Day play, and at the Blue Boar a scene of wild confusion reigned.

Tap-room and hall were crowded with guests, and in the cobbled court horses innumerable stamped and whinnied. The players, with knitted brows, stalked about the quieter nooks, going over their several parts, and looking to their costumes, which were for the most part upon their backs; while the thumping and pounding of the carpenters at work upon the stage in the inn-yard were enough to drive a quiet-loving person wild.

Nick Attwood scarcely knew whether he were on his head or on his heels. Carew, the master-player, would not let him eat at all after once breaking his fast, for fear it might affect his voice, and had him say his lines a hundred times until he had them pat. Then he was off, directing here, there, and everywhere, until the court was cleared of all that had no business there.

"Now, Nick," said Carew, coming up all in a gale, and throwing a sky-blue silken cloak about Nick's shoulders, "thou'lt enter here"; and he led him to a hallway door just opposite the gates. "When Master Whitelaw, as the Duke, calls out, 'How now, who comes?—I'll match him for the ale!' be quickly in and answer to thy part; and, marry, boy, don't miss thy cues, or—tsst, thy head's not worth a peascod!" With that he clapped his hand upon his poniard and glared into Nick's eyes, as if to look clear through to the back of the boy's wits. Nick heard his white teeth grind, and was all at once very much afraid of him, for he did indeed look dreadful.

So Nicholas Attwood stood by the entry door, with his heart in his throat, waiting his turn.

He could hear the pages in the courtyard outside shouting for stools for their masters, and squabbling over the best places upon the stage. Then the gates creaked, and there came a wild rush of feet and a great crying out as the 'prentices and burghers trooped into the inn-yard, pushing and crowding for places near the stage. Those who had the money bawled aloud for farthing stools. The rest stood jostling in a wrangling crowd upon the ground, while up and down a girl's shrill voice went all the time, crying high, "Cherry ripe, cherry ripe! Who'll buy my sweet May cherries?"

Then there was another shout, and a rattling tread of feet along the wooden balconies that ran around the walls of the inn-yard, and cries from the apprentices below: "Good-day, fair Master Harrington! Good-day, Sir Thomas Parkes! Good-day, sweet Mistress Nettleby and Master Nettleby! Good-day, good-day, good-day!" for the richer folk were coming in at twopence each, and all the galleries were full. And then he heard the baker's boy with sugared cakes and ginger-nuts go stamping up the stairs.

The musicians in the balcony overhead were tuning up. There was a flute, a viol, a gittern, a fiddle, and a drum; and behind the curtain, just outside the door, Nick could hear the master-player's low voice giving hasty orders to the others.

So he said his lines all over to himself, and cleared his throat. Then on a sudden a shutter opened high above the orchestra, a trumpet blared, the kettledrum crashed, and he heard a loud voice shout:

"Good citizens of Coventry, and high-born gentles all: know ye now that we, the players of the company of His Grace, Charles, Lord Howard, High Admiral of England, Ireland, Wales, Calais, and Boulogne, the marches of Normandy, Gascony, and Aquitaine, Captain-General of the Navy and the Seas of Her Gracious

98

Majesty the Queen—"

At that the crowd in the courtyard cheered and cheered again.

"—will, with your kind permission, play forthwith the laughable comedy of 'The Three Grey Gowns,' by Master Thomas Heywood, in which will be spoken many good things, old and new, and a brand-new song will be sung. Now, hearken all—the play begins!"

The trumpet blared, the kettledrum crashed again, and as a sudden hush fell over the throng without Nick heard the voices of the players going on.

It was a broad farce, full of loud jests and nonsense, a great thwacking of sticks and tumbling about; and Nick, with his eye to the crack of the door, listened with all his ears for his cue, far too excited even to think of laughing at the rough jokes, though the crowd in the inn-yard roared till they held their sides.

Carew came hurrying up, with an anxious look in his restless eyes.

"Ready, Nicholas!" said he, sharply, taking Nick by the arm and lifting the latch. "Go straight down front now as I told thee— mind thy cues—speak boldly—sing as thou didst sing for me— and if thou wouldst not break mine heart, do not fail me now!

I have staked it all upon thee here—and we *must* win!"

"How now, who comes?" Nick heard a loud voice call outside—the door-latch clicked behind him—he was out in the open
air and down the stage before he quite knew where he was.

The stage was built against the wall just opposite the gates. It
was but a temporary platform of planks laid upon trestles. One
side of it was against the wall, and around the three other sides
the crowd was packed close to the platform rail.

At the ends, upon the boards, several wealthy gallants sat on
high, three-legged stools, within arm's reach of the players acting
there. The courtyard was a sea of heads, and the balconies were
filled with gentlefolk in holiday attire, eating cakes and chaffing
gaily at the play. All was one bewildered cloud of staring eyes
to Nick, and the only thing which he was sure he saw was the
painted sign that hung upon the curtain at the rear, which in the
lack of other scenery announced in large red print: "This is a
Room in Master Jonah Jackdawe's House."

And then he heard the last quick words, "I'll match him for
the ale!" and started on his lines.

It was not that he said so ill what little he had to say, but that
his voice was homelike and familiar in its sound, one of their

own, with no amazing London accent to the words—just the speech of every-day, the sort that they all knew.

First, someone in the yard laughed out—a shock-headed iron-monger's apprentice, "Whoy, bullies, there be hayseed in his hair. 'Tis took off pasture over-soon. I fecks! they've plucked him green!"

There was a hoarse, exasperating laugh. Nick hesitated in his lines. The player at his back tried to prompt him, but only made the matter worse, and behind the green curtain at the door a hand went "clap" upon a dagger-hilt. The play lagged, and the crowd began to jeer. Nick's heart was full of fear and of angry shame that he had dared to try. Then all at once there came a brief pause, in which he vaguely realized that no one spoke. The man behind him thrust him forward, and whispering wrathfully, "Quick, quick—sing up, thou little fool!" stepped back and left him there alone.

A viol overhead took up the time, the gittern struck a few sharp notes. This unexpected music stopped the noise, and all was still. Nick thought of his mother's voice singing on a summer's evening among the hollyhocks, and as the viol's droning died away he drew a deep breath and began to sing the words of Heywood's newest song:

> "Pack, clouds, away, and welcome, day;
>   With night we banish sorrow;
> Sweet air, blow soft; mount, lark, aloft,
>   To give my love good-morrow!"

It was only a part of a madrigal, a simple strain, a few plain notes, and at the close one brief, queer, warbling trill like a bird's wild song, that rose and fell and rose again like a silver ripple.

The instruments were still; the fresh young voice came out alone, and it was done so soon that Nick hardly knew that he had sung at all. For a moment no one seemed to breathe. Then there was a very great noise, and all the court seemed hurling at him. A man upon the stage sprang to his feet. What they were going to do to him Nick did not know. He gave a frightened cry, and ran past the green curtain, through the open door, and into the master-player's excited arms.

"Quick, quick!" cried Carew. "Go back, go back! There, hark! —dost not hear them call? Quick, out again—they call thee back!" With that he thrust Nick through the door. The man upon the stage came up, slipped something into his hand—Nick, all be-

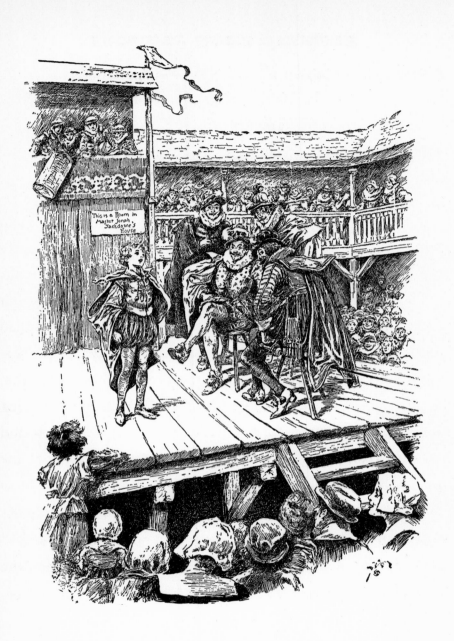

wildered, knew not what; and there he stood, quite stupefied, not knowing what to do. Then Carew came out hastily and led him down the stage, bowing, and pressing his hand to his heart, and smiling like a summer sunrise; so that Nick, seeing this, did the same, and bowed as neatly as he could; though, to be sure, his was only a simple, country-bred bow, and no such ceremonious to-do as Master Carew's courtly London obeisance.

Everyone was standing up and shouting so that not a soul could hear his ears, until the ironmonger's apprentice bellowed above the rest. "Whoy, bullies!" he shouted, amid a chorus of cheers and laughter, "didn't I say 'twas catched out in the fields—it be a skylark, sure enough! Come, Muster Skylark, sing that song again, an' thou shalt ha' my brand-new cap!"

Then many voices cried out together, "Sing it again! The Skylark—the Skylark!"

Nick looked up, startled. "Why, Master Carew," said he, with a tremble in his voice, "do they mean me?"

Carew put one hand beneath Nick's chin and turned his face up, smiling. The master-player's cheeks were flushed with triumph, and his dark eyes danced with pride. "Aye, Nicholas Skylark; 'tis thou they mean."

The viol and the music came again from overhead, and when they ceased Nick sang the little song once more. And when the master-player had taken him outside, and the play was over, some fine ladies came and kissed him, to his great confusion; for no one but his mother or his kin had ever done so before, and these had much perfume about them, musk and rose-attar, so that they smelled like rose-mallows in July. The players of the Lord Admiral's company were going about shaking hands with Carew and with each other as if they had not met for years, and slapping one another upon the back.

Nick then, for the first time, looked into his hand to see what the man upon the stage had given him. It was a gold rose-noble.

CAPTAIN'S SONG

from H.M.S. "PINAFORE"

by W. S. Gilbert

Capt. I am the Captain of the *Pinafore;*

All. And a right good captain, too!

Capt. You're very, very good,

And be it understood,

I command a right good crew,

All. We're very, very good,

And be it understood,

He commands a right good crew.

Capt. Though related to a peer,

I can hand, reef, and steer,

And ship a selvagee;

I am never known to quail

At the fury of a gale,

And I'm never, never sick at sea!

All. What, never?

Capt.   No, never!

All.   What, *never?*

Capt.   Hardly ever!

All.   He's hardly ever sick at sea!

Then give three cheers, and one cheer more,

For the hardy Captain of the *Pinafore!*

Capt. I do my best to satisfy you all—

All.   And with you we're quite content.

Capt.   You're exceedingly polite,

And I think it only right

To return the compliment.

All.   We're exceedingly polite,

And he thinks it's only right

To return the compliment.

Capt. Bad language or abuse

I never, never use,

Whatever the emergency;

Though "Bother it" I may

Occasionally say,

I never use a big, big D—

All.   What, never?

Capt.   No, never!

All.   What, *never?*

Capt.   Hardly ever!

All.   Hardly ever swears a big, big D—
          Then give three cheers, and one cheer more,
          For the well-bred Captain of the *Pinafore!*

THE DIVERTING HISTORY OF JOHN GILPIN

Showing How He Went Farther Than He Intended, and Came Safe
Home Again

by William Cowper

John Gilpin was a citizen
  Of credit and renown,
A train-band Captain eke was he
  Of famous London town.

John Gilpin's spouse said to her dear,
  "Though wedded we have been
These twice ten tedious years, yet we
  No holiday have seen.

Tomorrow is our wedding day,
  And we will then repair
Unto the Bell at Edmonton,
  All in a chaise and pair.

My sister and my sister's child,
   Myself and children three,
Will fill the chaise; so you must ride
   On horseback after we."

He soon replied, "I do admire
   Of womankind but one,
And you are she, my dearest dear,
   Therefore it shall be done.

I am a linen-draper bold,
   As all the world doth know,
And my good friend the Calender
   Will lend his horse to go."

Quoth Mrs. Gilpin, "That's well said,
   And for that wine is dear,
We will be furnish'd with our own,
   Which is both bright and clear."

John Gilpin kiss'd his loving wife;
   O'erjoyed was he to find
That though on pleasure she was bent,
   She had a frugal mind.

The morning came, the chaise was brought,
   But yet was not allow'd
To drive up to the door, lest all
   Should say that she was proud.

So three doors off the chaise was stay'd,
   Where they did all get in;
Six precious souls, and all agog
   To dash through thick and thin.

Smack went the whip, round went the wheels,
   Were never folk so glad.
The stones did rattle underneath
   As if Cheapside were mad.

John Gilpin at his horse's side,
　　Seized fast the flowing mane,
And up he got, in haste to ride,
　　But soon came down again;

For saddle-tree scarce reach'd had he,
　　His journey to begin,
When, turning round his head, he saw
　　Three customers come in.

So down he came; for loss of time,
　　Although it grieved him sore,
Yet loss of pence, full well he knew,
　　Would trouble him much more.

'Twas long before the customers
　　Were suited to their mind,
When Betty, screaming, came downstairs,
　　"The wine is left behind!"

"Good lack!" quoth he, "yet bring it me,
　　My leathern belt likewise,
In which I bear my trusty sword
　　When I do exercise."

Now Mistress Gilpin, careful soul,
　　Had two stone bottles found,
To hold the liquor that she loved,
　　And keep it safe and sound.

Each bottle had a curling ear,
　　Through which the belt he drew,
And hung a bottle on each side,
　　To make his balance true.

Then over all, that he might be
　　Equipp'd from top to toe,
His long red cloak, well brush'd and neat,
　　He manfully did throw.

Now see him mounted once again
   Upon his nimble steed,
Full slowly pacing o'er the stones
   With caution and good heed.

But, finding soon a smoother road
   Beneath his well-shod feet,
The snorting beast began to trot,
   Which gall'd him in his seat.

So "Fair and softly!" John he cried,
　　But John he cried in vain;
That trot became a gallop soon,
　　In spite of curb and rein.

So stooping down, as needs he must
　　Who cannot sit upright,
He grasp'd the mane with both his hands,
　　And eke with all his might.

His horse, who never in that sort
　　Had handled been before,
What thing upon his back had got
　　Did wonder more and more.

Away went Gilpin, neck or nought,
　　Away went hat and wig!
He little dreamt when he set out
　　Of running such a rig!

The wind did blow, the cloak did fly,
  Like streamer long and gay,
Till, loop and button failing both,
  At last it flew away.

Then might all people well discern
  The bottles he had slung;
A bottle swinging at each side,
  As hath been said or sung.

The dogs did bark, the children scream'd,
   Up flew the windows all,
And ev'ry soul cried out, "Well done!"
   As loud as he could bawl.

Away went Gilpin—who but he?
   His fame soon spread around—
"He carries weight!" "He rides a race!"
   " 'Tis for a thousand pound!"

And still, as fast as he drew near,
   'Twas wonderful to view,
How in a trice the turnpike-men
   Their gates wide open threw.

And now, as he went bowing down
   His reeking head full low,
The bottles twain behind his back
   Were shattered at a blow.

Down ran the wine into the road,
   Most piteous to be seen,
Which made his horse's flanks to smoke
   As they had basted been.

But still he seem'd to carry weight,
   With leathern girdle braced,
For all might see the bottle-necks
   Still dangling at his waist.

Thus all through merry Islington
   These gambols he did play,
Until he came unto the Wash
   Of Edmonton so gay.

And there he threw the Wash about
   On both sides of the way,
Just like unto a trundling mop,
   Or a wild-goose at play.

At Edmonton his loving wife
   From the balcony spied
Her tender husband, wond'ring much
   To see how he did ride.

"Stop, stop, John Gilpin!—Here's the house!"
   They all at once did cry;
"The dinner waits and we are tired."
   Said Gilpin—"So am I!"

But yet his horse was not a whit
   Inclined to tarry there;
For why? His owner had a house
   Full ten miles off, at Ware.

So like an arrow swift he flew,
   Shot by an archer strong;
So did he fly—which brings me to
   The middle of my song.

II

Away went Gilpin, out of breath,
   And sore against his will,
Till at his friend the Calender's
   His horse at last stood still.

The Calender, amazed to see
   His neighbor in such trim,
Laid down his pipe, flew to the gate,
   And thus accosted him:

"What news? What news? Your tidings tell,
   Tell me you must and shall—
Say why bare-headed you are come,
   Or why you come at all?"

Now Gilpin had a pleasant wit,
   And loved a timely joke,
And thus unto the Calender
   In merry guise he spoke:

"I came because your horse would come;
   And if I well forebode,
My hat and wig will soon be here,
   They are upon the road."

The Calender, right glad to find
   His friend in merry pin,
Return'd him not a single word,
   But to the house went in;

Whence straight he came with hat and wig,
   A wig that flow'd behind,
A hat not much the worse for wear,
   Each comely in its kind.

He held them up, and in his turn
   Thus show'd his ready wit:
"My head is twice as big as yours,
   They therefore needs must fit.

But let me scrape the dirt away
   That hangs upon your face;
And stop and eat, for well you may
   Be in a hungry case."

Said John, "It is my wedding-day,
   And all the world would stare,
If wife should dine at Edmonton,
   And I should dine at Ware."

So, turning to his horse, he said—
   "I am in haste to dine;
'Twas for your pleasure you came here,
   You shall go back for mine."

Ah, luckless speech and bootless boast!
   For which he paid full dear;
For, while he spake, a braying ass
   Did sing most loud and clear;

Whereat his horse did snort, as he
　　Had heard a lion roar,
And gallop'd off with all his might,
　　As he had done before.

Away went Gilpin, and away
   Went Gilpin's hat and wig!
He lost them sooner than at first,
   For why?—They were too big!

Now Mistress Gilpin, when she saw
   Her husband posting down
Into the country far away,
   She pull'd out half-a-crown;

And thus unto the youth she said
   That drove them to the Bell—
"This shall be yours when you bring back
   My husband safe and well."

The youth did ride, and soon did meet
   John coming back amain;
Whom in a trice he tried to stop,
   By catching at his rein;

But not performing what he meant,
    And gladly would have done,
The frighted steed he frighted more,
    And made him faster run.

Away went Gilpin, and away
    Went post-boy at his heels!
The post-boy's horse right glad to miss
    The lumb'ring of the wheels.

Six gentlemen upon the road
    Thus seeing Gilpin fly,
With post-boy scamp'ring in the rear,
    They raised the hue and cry:

"Stop thief! Stop thief! A highwayman!"
    Not one of them was mute.
And all and each that pass'd that way
    Did join in the pursuit.

And now the turnpike gates again
  Flew open in short space;
The toll-men thinking, as before,
  That Gilpin rode a race.

And so he did, and won it too,
    For he got first to town;
Nor stopp'd till where he had got up
    He did again get down.

Now let us sing, Long live the king,
    And Gilpin, long live he;
And when he next doth ride abroad,
    May I be there to see!

THE LITTLE PRINCESS AND BECKY

from THE LITTLE PRINCESS

by Frances Hodgson Burnett

THE LITTLE PRINCESS AND BECKY

THE GREATEST power Sara possessed was her power of telling stories and of making everything she talked about seem like a story, whether it was one or not.

Anyone who has been at school with a teller of stories knows what the wonder means—how he or she is followed about and besought in a whisper to relate romances; how groups gather round and hang on the outskirts of the favored party in the hope of being allowed to join it and listen. Sara not only could tell stories, but she adored telling them. When she sat or stood in the midst of a circle and began to invent wonderful things, her green eyes grew big and shining, her cheeks flushed, and, without knowing that she was doing it, she began to act and made what she told lovely or alarming by the raising or dropping of her voice, the bend and sway of her slim body, and the dramatic movement of her hands. She forgot that she was talking to listening children; she saw and lived with the fairy folk, or the kings and queens and beautiful ladies, whose adventures she was narrating. Some-

135

times when she had finished her story, she was quite out of breath with excitement, and would lay her hand on her thin, little, quick-rising chest, and half laugh as if at herself.

"When I am telling it," she would say, "it doesn't seem as if it was only made up. It seems more real than you are—more real than the school-room. I feel as if I were all the people in the story —one after the other. It *is* queer."

She had been at Miss Minchin's school about two years when, one foggy winter's afternoon, as she was getting out of her carriage, she caught sight, as she crossed the pavement, of a dingy little figure standing on the area steps, and stretching its neck so that its wide-open eyes might peer at her through the railings. Something in the eagerness and timidity of the smudgy face made her look at it, and when she looked she smiled because it was her way to smile at people.

But the owner of the smudgy face and the wide-open eyes evidently was afraid that she ought not to have been caught looking at pupils of importance. She dodged out of sight like a Jack-in-the-box and scurried back into the kitchen, disappearing so suddenly that if she had not been such a poor, little forlorn thing, Sara would have laughed in spite of herself. That very evening, as Sara was sitting in the midst of a group of listeners in a corner of the school-room telling one of her stories, the very same figure timidly entered the room, carrying a coal-box much too heavy for her, and knelt down upon the hearth-rug to replenish the fire and sweep up the ashes.

She was cleaner than she had been when she peeped through the area railings, but she looked just as frightened. She was evidently afraid to look at the children or seem to be listening. She put on pieces of coal cautiously with her fingers so that she might make no disturbing noise, and she swept about the fire-irons very softly. But Sara saw in two minutes that she was deeply interested in what was going on, and that she was doing her work slowly in the hope of catching a word here and there. And realizing this, she raised her voice and spoke more clearly.

"The Mermaids swam softly about in the crystal-green water, and dragged after them a fishing-net woven of deep-sea pearls," she said. "The Princess sat on the white rock and watched them."

It was a wonderful story about a princess who was loved by a Prince Merman, and went to live with him in shining caves under the sea.

The small drudge before the grate swept the hearth once and

then swept it again. Having done it twice, she did it three times; and, as she was doing it the third time, the sound of the story so lured her to listen that she fell under the spell and actually forgot that she had no right to listen at all, and also forgot everything else. She sat down upon her heels as she knelt on the hearth-rug, and the brush hung idly in her fingers. The voice of the story-teller went on and drew her with it into winding grottos under the sea, glowing with soft, clear blue light, and paved with pure golden sands. Strange sea flowers and grasses waved about her, and far away faint singing and music echoed.

The hearth-brush fell from the work-roughened hand, and Lavinia Herbert looked around.

"That girl has been listening," she said.

The culprit snatched up her brush, and scrambled to her feet. She caught at the coal-box and simply scuttled out of the room like a frightened rabbit.

"Who is that little girl who makes the fires?" Sara asked Mariette that night.

Mariette broke forth into a flow of description.

Ah, indeed, Mademoiselle Sara might well ask. She was a forlorn little thing who had just taken the place of scullery-maid—

138

though, as to being scullery-maid, she was everything else besides. She blacked boots and grates, and carried heavy coal-scuttles up and down stairs, and scrubbed floors and cleaned windows, and was ordered about by everybody. She was fourteen years old, but was so stunted in growth that she looked about twelve. In truth, Mariette was sorry for her. She was so timid that if one chanced to speak to her it appeared as if her poor, frightened eyes would jump out of her head.

"What is her name?" asked Sara, who had sat by the table, with her chin on her hands, as she listened absorbedly to the recital.

Her name was Becky. Mariette heard everyone below-stairs calling, "Becky, do this," and "Becky, do that," every five minutes in the day.

Sara sat and looked into the fire, reflecting on Becky for some time after Mariette left her. She made up a story of which Becky was the ill-used heroine. She thought she looked as if she had never had quite enough to eat. Her very eyes were hungry. She hoped she should see her again, but though she caught sight of her carrying things up or down stairs on several occasions, she always seemed in such a hurry and so afraid of being seen that it was impossible to speak to her.

But a few weeks later, on another foggy afternoon, when she entered her sitting-room she found herself confronting a rather pathetic picture. In her own special and pet easy-chair before the bright fire, Becky—with a coal smudge on her nose and several on her apron, with her poor little cap hanging half off her head, and an empty coal-box on the floor near her—sat fast asleep, tired out beyond even the endurance of her hard-working young body. She had been sent up to put the bedrooms in order for the evening. There were a great many of them, and she had been running about all day. Sara's rooms she had saved until the last. They were not like the other rooms, which were plain and bare. Ordinary pupils were expected to be satisfied with mere necessaries. Sara's comfortable sitting-room seemed a bower of luxury to the scullery-maid, though it was, in fact, merely a nice, bright little room. But there were pictures and books in it, and curious things from India; there was a sofa and the low, soft chair; and there was always a glowing fire and a polished grate. Becky saved it until the end of her afternoon's work, because it rested her to go into it, and she always hoped to snatch a few minutes to sit down in the soft chair and look about her, and think about the wonder-

ful good fortune of the child who owned such surroundings and who went out on the cold days in beautiful hats and coats one tried to catch a glimpse of through the area railing.

On this afternoon, when she had sat down, the sensation of relief to her short, aching legs had been so wonderful and delightful that it had seemed to soothe her whole body, and the glow of warmth and comfort from the fire had crept over her like a spell, until, as she looked at the red coals, a tired, slow smile stole over her smudged face, her head nodded forward without her being aware of it, her eyes drooped, and she fell fast asleep. She had really been only about ten minutes in the room when Sara entered, but she was in as deep a sleep as if she had been, like the Sleeping Beauty, slumbering for a hundred years. But she did not look—poor Becky!—like a Sleeping Beauty at all. She looked only like an ugly, stunted, worn-out little scullery drudge.

Sara seemed as much unlike her as if she were a creature from another world.

On this particular afternoon she had been taking her dancing-lesson, and the afternoon on which the dancing-master appeared was rather a grand occasion at the seminary, though it occurred every week. The pupils were attired in their prettiest frocks, and as Sara danced particularly well, she was very much brought forward, and Mariette was requested to make her as diaphanous and fine as possible.

Today a frock the color of a rose had been put on her, and Mariette had bought some real buds and made her a wreath to wear on her black locks. She had been learning a new, delightful dance in which she had been skimming and flying about the room, like a large rose-colored butterfly, and the enjoyment and exercise had brought a brilliant, happy glow into her face.

When she entered the room, she floated in with a few of the butterfly steps—and there sat Becky, nodding her cap sideways off her head.

"Oh!" cried Sara, softly, when she saw her. "That poor thing!"

It did not occur to her to feel cross at finding her pet chair occupied by the small, dingy figure. To tell the truth, she was quite glad to find it there. When the ill-used heroine of her story wakened, she could talk to her. She crept toward her quietly, and stood looking at her. Becky gave a little snore.

"I wish she'd waken herself," Sara said. "I don't like to waken her. But Miss Minchin would be cross if she found out. I'll just wait a few minutes."

She took a seat on the edge of the table, and sat swinging her slim, rose-colored legs, and wondering what it would be best to do. Miss Amelia might come in at any moment, and if she did, Becky would be sure to be scolded.

"But she is so tired," she thought. "She *is* so tired!"

A piece of flaming coal ended her perplexity for her that very moment. It broke off from a large lump and fell on to the fender. Becky started, and opened her eyes with a frightened gasp. She did not know she had fallen asleep. She had only just sat down for one moment and felt the beautiful glow—and here she found herself staring in wild alarm at the wonderful pupil, who sat perched quite near her, like a rose-colored fairy, with interested eyes.

She sprang up and clutched at her cap. She felt it dangling over her ear, and tried wildly to put it straight. Oh, she had got herself into trouble now with a vengeance! To have impudently fallen asleep on such a young lady's chair! She would be turned out of doors without wages.

She made a sound like a big breathless sob.

"Oh, miss! Oh, miss!" she stuttered. "I arst yer pardon, miss! Oh, I do, miss!"

Sara jumped down, and came quite close to her.

"Don't be frightened," she said, quite as if she had been speaking to a little girl like herself. "It doesn't matter the least bit."

"I didn't go to do it, miss," protested Becky. "It was the warm fire—an' me bein' so tired. It—it *wasn't* imperence!"

Sara broke into a friendly little laugh, and put her hand on her shoulder.

"You were tired," she said; "you could not help it. You are not really awake yet."

How poor Becky stared at her! In fact, she had never heard such a nice, friendly sound in anyone's voice before. She was used to being ordered about and scolded, and having her ears boxed. And this one—in her rose-colored dancing afternoon splendor—was looking at her as if she were not a culprit at all—as if she had a right to be tired—even to fall asleep! The touch of the soft, slim little paw on her shoulder was the most amazing thing she had ever known.

"Ain't—ain't yer angry, miss?" she gasped. "Ain't yer goin' to tell the missus?"

"No," cried out Sara. "Of course I'm not."

The woeful fright in the coal-smutted face made her suddenly so sorry that she could scarcely bear it. One of her queer thoughts rushed into her mind. She put her hand against Becky's cheek.

"Why," she said, "we are just the same—I am only a little girl like you. It's just an accident that I am not you, and you are not me!"

Becky did not understand in the least. Her mind could not grasp such amazing thoughts, and "an accident" meant to her a calamity in which someone was run over or fell off a ladder and was carried to "the 'orspital."

"A' accident, miss," she fluttered respectfully. "Is it?"

"Yes," Sara answered, and she looked at her dreamily for a moment. But the next she spoke in a different tone. She realized that Becky did not know what she meant.

"Have you done your work?" she asked. "Dare you stay here a few minutes?"

Becky lost her breath again.

"Here, miss? Me?"

Sara ran to the door, opened it, and looked out and listened.

"No one is anywhere about," she explained. "If your bedrooms are finished, perhaps you might stay a tiny while. I thought—perhaps—you might like a piece of cake."

The next ten minutes seemed to Becky like a sort of delirium. Sara opened a cupboard, and gave her a thick slice of cake. She seemed to rejoice when it was devoured in hungry bites. She talked and asked questions, and laughed until Becky's fears actually began to calm themselves, and she once or twice gathered boldness enough to ask a question or so herself, daring as she felt it to be.

"Is that—" she ventured, looking longingly at the rose-colored frock. And she asked it almost in a whisper. "Is that there your best?"

"It is one of my dancing-frocks," answered Sara. "I like it, don't you?"

For a few seconds Becky was almost speechless with admiration. Then she said in an awed voice:

"Onct I see a princess. I was standin' in the street with the crowd outside Covin' Garden, watchin' the swells go inter the operer. An' there was one everyone stared at most. They ses to each other, 'That's the princess.' She was a growed-up young lady, but she was pink all over—gownd an' cloak, an' flowers an' all. I called her to mind the minnit I see you, sittin' there on the table, miss. You looked like her."

"I've often thought," said Sara, in her reflecting voice, "that I should like to be a princess; I wonder what it feels like. I believe I will begin pretending I am one."

Becky stared at her admiringly, and, as before, did not understand her in the least. She watched her with a sort of adoration. Very soon Sara left her reflections and turned to her with a new question.

"Becky," she said, "weren't you listening to that story?"

"Yes, miss," confessed Becky, a little alarmed again. "I knowed I hadn't orter, but it was that beautiful I—I couldn't help it."

"I liked you to listen to it," said Sara. "If you tell stories, you like nothing so much as to tell them to people who want to listen. I don't know why it is. Would you like to hear the rest?"

Becky lost her breath again.

"Me hear it?" she cried. "Like as if I was a pupil, miss! All about the Prince—and the little white Mer-babies swimming about laughing—with stars in their hair?"

Sara nodded.

"You haven't time to hear it now, I'm afraid," she said; "but if you will tell me just what time you come to do my rooms, I will try to be here and tell you a bit of it every day until it is finished.

It's a lovely long one—and I'm always putting new bits to it."

"Then," breathed Becky, devoutly, "I wouldn't mind *how* heavy the coal-boxes was—or *what* the cook done to me, if—if I might have that to think of."

"You may," said Sara. "I'll tell it *all* to you."

When Becky went down-stairs, she was not the same Becky who had staggered up, loaded down by the weight of the coal-scuttle. She had an extra piece of cake in her pocket, and she had been fed and warmed, but not only by cake and fire. Something else had warmed and fed her, and the something else was Sara.

THE GRUMPITY MAN

Hoighty, toighty, grumpity man!
Finding fault since your life began!
Pity we haven't a comet or two
To carry off passengers such as you!

WISHES

by Florence E. Pratt

A Reginald Birch little boy
   Met the sweetest of Greenaway girls;
She, dressed all in Puritan brown,
   He, with cavalier ruffles and curls.

Her eyes were of solemnest brown,
   Her hair was cropped close to her head.
His curls were a riot of gold,
   His cheeks were of healthiest red.

They looked at each other awhile,
   Gay gallant and Puritan maid;
Then the Reginald Birch little boy
   Slowly and solemnly said:

"I wish *you* wore rufflety clothes!
I wish that *my* hair was cut short!
'Cause the boys call me 'missy' and 'girl,'
And it interferes so with my sport."

Said she, "Oh, I like pretty clothes,
    And I *do* wish they'd let my hair curl!
I wish *you* were a Greenaway boy,
    And I was a Fauntleroy girl!"

THE OWL AND THE PUSSY-CAT

by Edward Lear

The Owl and the Pussy-Cat went to sea
   In a beautiful pea-green boat:
They took some honey, and plenty of money
   Wrapped up in a five-pound note.

154

The Owl looked up to the stars above,
　And sang to a small guitar,
"O lovely Pussy, O Pussy, my love,
　What a beautiful Pussy you are,
　　　　You are,
　　　　You are!
What a beautiful Pussy you are!"

Pussy said to the Owl, "You elegant fowl,
   How charmingly sweet you sing!
Oh, let us be married; too long we have tarried!
   But what shall we do for a ring?"
They sailed away, for a year and a day,
   To the land where the bong-tree grows;
And there in a wood a Piggy-wig stood,
   With a ring at the end of his nose,
       His nose,
       His nose,
With a ring at the end of his nose.

"Dear Pig, are you willing to sell for one shilling
   Your ring?" Said the Piggy, "I will."
So they took it away, and were married next day
   By the turkey who lives on the hill.
They dined on mince and slices of quince,
   Which they ate with a runcible spoon;

And hand in hand, on the edge of the sand,
They danced by the light of the moon,
The moon,
The moon,
They danced by the light of the moon.

THE DRAGON AND THE DRAGOON
by Tudor Jenks

THE DRAGON AND THE DRAGOON

THERE WAS once a prosperous little town that grew up in a valley shut in by high mountains. A road entered the valley by a narrow rocky pass at one end, ran through the town, making the chief street, and then climbed the mountains and led out of the valley again. There was no way through the valley except by this road.

As the road was a highway between two large cities, the valley town became a convenient resting-place for traders and travelers, and profited by their custom.

Far up on one of the mountains overhanging the valley lived a colony of dragons. They were very timid creatures, and, remaining amid the rocky heights of their home, were never seen by men. Indeed, the inhabitants of the valley would have said there were no such creatures in existence. But as the dragons were not disturbed they increased in numbers, and soon found it a difficult matter to secure food. Then the stronger dragons drove their weaker fellows away from their native places, compelling them to seek a living elsewhere.

One young dragon happened at last to station himself in one of the passes that led into the valley where the town was situated; and, being tired by his long crawl, the dragon lay down in the highway to rest.

Soon there came a party of traders, on foot and horseback, making their way toward the town, where they expected to rest that night. While jogging along quietly, talking about the equator, suddenly they found themselves face to face with the young dragon.

There were seven travelers, and they gave seven different sorts of yell, threw down their bundles, and took to their own or their horses' heels, without arranging where to meet again.

Now it happened, the dragon being greenish in hue, that he had not been seen until the party of traders was just opposite; and consequently the fleeing traders separated into two parties. Four of them ran back toward the city they had left that morning, and three went helter-skelter down into the valley town.

As for the dragon, he was more scared than anybody; and he tried to run away too. But, being in too much of a hurry to climb either side of the pass, he ran first after one party, and then after the other. Finding men in both directions, he returned and howled

dismally.

But when the poor thing's terror had worn itself out, he began to nose about among those packages the travelers had thrown away. He found several packages of raisins, three or four hams, some salted fish, and a small keg of ginger. He was very hungry, and devoured all this food without thinking of his digestion, and soon after sank into an unquiet slumber.

Meanwhile the seven travelers were relating to the citizens and villagers the awful adventure that had befallen them in the pass. The seven travelers told seven different stories, and their listeners, in carrying the report to their neighbors, freely invented whatever small details each found necessary. So by nightfall nearly every household had scared itself out of its seven senses with a mixture of a little fact and a great deal of guessing. By midnight both town and city were either dozing uneasily or were staring wide awake with ears pricked up.

And by midnight that unhappy dragon was wide awake, too, and struggling with a severe internal pain. As his diet until then had been mainly mountain herbs and spring water, it is not surprising that the miscellaneous bill of fare he had just eaten should disagree with him.

The dragon did not understand what was the trouble, but he soon began to yell and roar and whine and grumble.

Down in the valley below these noises rose upon the night air with a soul-freezing effect, and those citizens who had first said "Pooh!" or "Pshaw—nonsense!" were scared out of their seven wits.

The next day the Mayor summoned the town-council, and held a meeting behind locked doors. The councilmen were staid, respectable merchants, but they came into the Town Hall shaking in their shoes.

"Gentlemen," said the Mayor, "an unfounded rumor has come to our ears—"

Just then a wild shriek was heard faintly in the distance, and the Mayor stopped short, turned pale, and remained silent until the echoes died away. Then he began again:

"Gentlemen—this most extraordinary occurrence, of which no doubt—" here a second wail of distress made him catch his breath; and the Mayor abruptly concluded, "How are we to get rid of this frightful creature?"

After a few moments one of the council rose and remarked as follows:

"There is no danger, I have understood, so long as the dragon is well fed. If the beast is made desperate by hunger, he may be tempted to descend into the town, and who can tell—" a third yell rose, swelled to a shriek, and died away—"who can tell, I say, what awful things he may do?"

"What can be done?" asked the Mayor.

"I advise that we send the militia with a store of provisions, and let them deposit these in the road, so the monster may not approach."

Since no other plan was proposed, a vote was taken, and the measure was adopted unanimously.

The militia grumbled, but they had to go. Armed to the teeth, they started up toward the pass, accompanied by two very heavily loaded wagons containing a choice selection of provisions. As the dragon was now feeling less disturbed, his complaints had ceased; and the militia gained in courage as they advanced. They saw no signs of the dragon, and began to believe he had fled. But when they had come near enough to see the traders' baggage torn to bits, they lost courage at once, and, wheeling to the right-about, began a return march that soon became a retreat, then turned into a rout, and ended in a panic. They arrived in town in single

file; the best runner first, the second next, and so on down to the drummer-boy, a little fellow who couldn't get up much speed, and who ran only because the rest did.

As the wagons had been cut loose and left in the road, it was not long before the dragon discovered them. When his appetite returned, he examined the contents of the two wagons, helped himself freely, and, before many hours had passed, was again in trouble with himself, and again confiding his troubles to the mountain echoes.

When the dragon's roaring was heard for the second time, the Mayor, without waiting to convene his advisers, sent a second supply of food.

This time the soldiers didn't go further than was necessary to see the other wagons. Consequently the dragon, gaining in courage and confidence, came nearer to the town, and made a third meal.

This time, the drummer-boy, who was a brave little fellow after all, became rather curious about the dragon. Instead of running away, therefore, he waited until the rest of the troop were out of sight, and then climbed a tree.

For a while nothing happened; and the drummer-boy began

even to get sleepy; but just about twilight the boy heard the rattling and crackling of the dragon's scales. He peered out through the leaves and soon saw the dragon cautiously crawling down the road toward the wagons. The boy was so startled by the sight that he gave a violent jump, and thereby knocked his drum out of its resting-place in the tree.

Whack-bang—rattlety—bang! the drum fell through the branches to the ground. And at the noise the timid dragon went scuttling away up the road like a frightened mouse.

"Oho!" cried the boy. "So that's the sort of a creature you are, Mr. Dragon!"

Climbing leisurely down, the drummer-boy picked up his drum, slung it over his shoulder, and returned to the town, laughing quietly to himself.

But when, the next day, the dragon made a new disturbance, he was so much nearer the town that there was consternation among the citizens. They ran to the Town Hall in throngs, and insisted that measures be taken either to destroy the monster or to protect the town from his nearer approach.

After a stormy meeting at the Town Hall, the town-crier appeared and read a proclamation from the Mayor offering a rich reward to whoever could "devise, invent, or contrive" some effective "means, plan, or contrivance" that would now, "henceforth and forevermore" and "without fail put an end to and abate" the "said public menace, enemy, and threat to the prosperity and welfare of the municipality."

The proclamation, in fact, wound up by promising to grant any request that might be made by the lucky man who should succeed in overcoming or getting rid of the dragon.

No sooner was the proclamation read than the drummer-boy darted out from the crier's audience and sped away home as fast as he could go. For the drummer-boy had a big brother, and the Mayor had a daughter, and the big brother was in love with the Mayor's daughter, who was a lovely and accomplished young lady. But the Mayor had frowned upon the big brother's suit, because the young man was only a lieutenant of dragoons, instead of a brigadier-general glittering with gold lace, with epaulets, and other trimmings.

The drummer-boy hastened home and ran up to his brother's room. The big brother was trying to write verses, and making himself sadder because the verses were not proving all that he tried to make them. And the drummer-boy rushed in, and forgot

to knock at the door, and began to tell his big brother all about the Mayor and the proclamation, and the dragon, and the drum falling out of the tree, and the dragon's running away, until the big brother was entirely bewildered.

But after a while the drummer-boy succeeded in telling his story, and the big brother succeeded in understanding it. And then both put on their best hats, and ran off to the Mayor's house. They rang the bell hard, were admitted, and the lieutenant offered to rid the town of the dragon upon condition that the Mayor would promise him his chosen bride. The Mayor was not at all impressed; but he made up his mind that either the young lieutenant of dragoons would succeed in driving off the dragon, or else that the dragon would take care that he was no more bothered by the lieutenant. So he agreed to the plan, put his promise in writing, sealed it with his signet-ring, and dismissed the two with a feeling of relief.

Next day the lieutenant and the drummer-boy set forth for the pass. They were armed only with a few giant firecrackers and a supply of matches.

When they reached the pass, the dragon, who had learned to expect food when he saw uniforms approaching, came smilingly forward to meet them. The big brother was a little nervous, perhaps; and so, when the dragon came within about a hundred yards, he lighted one of the cannon-crackers, and flung it toward the dragon.

Now, the dragon expected food; and when he saw the attractive red-paper covering of the cracker, he rushed forward, and caught it eagerly in his mouth. The dragon tried to bite the cracker in two; but there was no need of that—the giant cracker came to pieces without any assistance, and the dragon was frightened almost to death by the noise of the explosion and the terrific concussion. He started to run away up the pass. But the drummer-boy had meanwhile lighted another firecracker; and this was thrown so cleverly that it exploded just in front of the fleeing dragon.

Then, with an awful shriek, the dragon turned and went climbing up over the rocks. But before he could get away, the lieutenant was after him; and, overtaking the scared reptile, he seized him by the tail.

The dragon fainted from terror.

Convinced now that the dragon was an arrant coward, the lieutenant and the drummer-boy cut two stout sticks, and when the dragon had recovered his senses they drove him through the town and into their back yard.

So it all ended happily. The dragon was fed upon oatmeal and rice-pudding until he was quite amiable. The lieutenant married the Mayor's daughter, and was made Generalissimo and Commander-in-chief of all the forces, and the drummer-boy was appointed Drum-major for life, with a pension for old age. And I must say that I wish all stories turned out as satisfactorily for all concerned.

SONG OF THE GRAND INQUISITOR

from THE GONDOLIERS

by W. S. Gilbert

I stole the Prince, and brought him here,
  And left him gaily prattling
With a highly respectable gondolier,
Who promised the Royal babe to rear,
And teach him the trade of a timoneer
  With his own beloved bratling.

    Both of the babes were strong and stout,
      And, considering all things, clever.
    Of that there is no manner of doubt—
    No probable, possible shadow of doubt—
    No possible doubt whatever.

But owing, I'm much disposed to fear,
  To his terrible taste for tippling,
That highly respectable gondolier

Could never declare with a mind sincere
Which of the two was his offspring dear,
  And which the Royal stripling!

Which was which he could never make out
    Despite his best endeavor.
Of *that* there is no manner of doubt—
No probable, possible shadow of doubt—
    No possible doubt whatever.

Time sped, and when at the end of a year
    I sought that infant cherished,
That highly respectable gondolier
Was lying a corpse on his humble bier—
I dropped a Grand Inquisitor's tear—
    That gondolier had perished.

A taste for drink combined with gout,
    Had doubled him up for ever.
Of *that* there is no manner of doubt—
No probable, possible shadow of doubt—
    No possible doubt whatever.

The children followed his old career—
  (This statement can't be parried)
Of a highly respectable gondolier:
Well, one of the two (who will soon be here)—
But *which* of the two is not quite clear—
  Is the Royal Prince you married!

    Search in and out and round about,
      And you'll discover never
    A tale so free from every doubt—
    All probable, possible shadow of doubt—
      All possible doubt whatever!

WHAT THE LORD HIGH CHAMBERLAIN SAID

by Virginia Woodward Cloud

Little Prince Carl he stole away
  From the gold-laced guard and the powdered page,
And the ladies in waiting, who night and day
  Kept their bird in a gilded cage.

Alone in the twilight gray and dim,
  He climbed on the carven chair of state,
And there with a smile sufficiently grim,
  And a royal air, His Highness sate.

He folded his arms with a mighty mien,—
  Little Prince Carl, the son of a king,—
But never an auditor was to be seen,
  Save the pea-green cockatoo, perched in his swing!

And rebellion shone in His Highness' eyes:
  "When I am a king full-grown," said he,
"I fear there is going to be surprise
  At some of the things this court shall see!

180

"With the Dowager Duchess I shall begin;
   When I say, 'Stand forth!' she shall bow her low.
'For me to jump you have said was a sin;
   I command *you* to jump wherever you go!'

182

"The Court Physician I next shall take:
 'And you, I hear, have declared it best
That I, your monarch, shall not eat cake,—
 Plum-cake, too, of the very best!—

183

" 'Well, *you* are to eat a gallon of rice,
   And nothing besides, for every meal;
I am sure 'tis quite "wholesome," "nourishing," "nice,"
   But I know quite well just how you feel!'

"Now let the Lord Chamberlain have a care!"
   His Highness' voice took a terrible ring;
He rumpled his curls of yellow hair,
   And the pea-green cockatoo shook in its swing!

" 'Down! Get down on your knocking knees,
   Down with your smile and your snuff-box, too!'
I will thunder, 'and now 'tis time, if you please,
   To settle an old, old score with you!

" 'What became of those three white mice
   That crept from the royal nursery door,
After you said if they did it twice
   They should never be heard of any more?

184

" '*I know, for I heard the little one squeak!*
   And I ran and stopped my ears up tight.
You need not squirm, and you need not speak,
   For your fate shall be settled this very night.

" 'In the darkest depths of the dungeon lone
   You are to live; but do not fear,
For company livelier than your own
   You shall have three million mice a year!' "

The little Prince clapped his hands in glee,
   And laughed aloud at this fancying,—
Oh, a rare and a wonderful monarch he!—
   And the pea-green cockatoo hopped in its swing:

When out of the twilight a slow voice rolled;
   There stood the High Chamberlain, stern, who said:
"I regret to state that I've just been told
   It is time for Your Highness to go to bed!"

And lo! not a word did His Highness say!—
He went at once, like the son of a king.
But his bright curls drooped as he walked away,
And the cockatoo's head went under its wing.

THE CASTLE OF BIM

from THE REFORMED PIRATE

by Frank R. Stockton

THE CASTLE OF BIM

LORIS was a little girl, about eleven years old, who lived with her father, in a very small house among the mountains of a distant land. He was sometimes a wood-cutter, and sometimes a miner, or a plowman, or a stone-breaker. Being an industrious man he would work at anything he could do when a chance offered, but as there was not much work to do in that part of the country, poor Jorn often found it very hard to make a living for himself and Loris.

One day, when he had gone out early to look for work, Loris was in her little sleeping-room under the roof, braiding her hair. Although she was so poor, Loris always tried to make herself look as neat as she could, for that pleased her father. She was just tying the ribbon on the end of the long braid, when she heard a knock at the door below. "In one second," she said to herself, "I will go. I must tie this ribbon tightly, for it would never do to lose it."

And so she tied it, and ran down-stairs to the door; there was no one there.

"Oh, it is too bad!" cried Loris. "Perhaps it was someone with a job for father. He told me always to be very careful about answering a knock at the door, for there was no knowing when someone might come with a good job, and now someone has come, and gone," cried Loris, looking about in every direction for the person who had knocked. "Oh, there he is! How could he have got away so far in such a short time? I must run after him."

So away she ran as fast as she could, after a man she saw, walking away from the cottage in the direction of a forest.

"Oh, dear!" she said, as she ran. "How fast he walks! and he is such a short man, too! He is going right to the hut of Laub, that wicked Laub, who is always trying to get away work from father, and he came first to our house, but thought there was nobody at home."

Loris ran and ran, but the short man did walk very fast. However, she gradually gained on him, and just as he reached Laub's door, she seized him by the coat. "Stop—sir, please," she said, scarcely able to speak, she was so out of breath. The man turned and looked at her. He was a very short man indeed, for he scarcely reached to Loris' waist.

"What do you want?" he said, looking up at her.

"Oh, sir!" she gasped, "you came to our house first—and I came to the door—almost as quick as I could—and if it's any work—father wants work—ever so bad."

"Yes," said the short man, "but Laub wants work too. He is very poor."

"Yes, sir," said Loris, "but—but you came for father first."

"True," said the short man, "but nobody answered my knock, and now I am here. Laub has four young children, and sometimes they have nothing to eat. It is never so bad with you, is it?"

"No, sir," said Loris.

"Your father has work sometimes, is it not so?"

"Yes, sir," answered Loris.

"Laub is often without work for weeks, and he has four children. Shall I go back with you or knock here?"

"Knock," said Loris softly.

The short man knocked at the door, and instantly there was heard a great scuffling and hubbub within. Shortly all was quiet, and then a voice said, "Come in."

"He did not wait so long for me," thought Loris.

The short man opened the door and went in, Loris following him. In a bed, in the corner of the room, were four children; their heads just appearing above a torn sheet which was pulled up to their chins.

"Hello! what's the matter?" said the short man, advancing to the bed.

"Please, sir," said the oldest child, a girl of about the age of Loris, with tangled hair and sharp black eyes, "we are all sick, and very poor, and our father has no work. If you can give us a little money to buy bread—"

"All sick, eh!" said the short man. "Any particular disease?"

"We don't know about diseases, sir," said the girl, "we've never been to school."

"No doubt of that," said the man. "I have no money to give you, but you can tell your father that if he will come to the mouth of the Ragged Mine, tomorrow morning, he can have a job of work which will pay him well." So saying he went out. Loris followed him, but he simply waved his hand to her, and in a few minutes was lost in the forest.

Loris looked sadly after him, and then walked slowly towards her home.

The moment their visitors had gone, the Laub children sprang out of bed, as lively as crickets.

194

"Ha! Ha!" cried the oldest girl. "She came after him to get it, and he wouldn't give it to her, and father's got it. Served her right, the horrid thing!" and all the children shouted, "Horrid thing!" One of the boys now ran out, and threw a stone after Loris, and then they sat down to finish eating a meat-pie, which had been given them.

"Well," said Jorn that evening when Loris told him what had happened. "I'm sorry, for I found but little work today, but it can't be helped. You did all you could."

"No, father," said Loris. "I might have gone to the door quicker."

"That may be," said Jorn, "and I hope you will never keep anyone waiting again."

Two or three days after this, as Loris was stooping over the fire, in the back room of the cottage, preparing her dinner, she heard a knock.

Springing to her feet, she dropped the pan she held in her hand, and made a dash at the front door, pulling it open with a tremendous fling. No one should go away this time.

"Hello! Ho! Ho!" cried a person outside, giving a skip backwards. "Do you open doors by lightning here?"

"No, sir," said Loris; "but I didn't want to keep you waiting."

"I should think not," said the other; "why, I had hardly begun to knock."

This visitor was a middle-sized man, very slight, and, at first sight, of a youthful appearance. But his hair was either powdered or gray, and it was difficult to know whether he was old or young. His face was long and smooth, and he nearly always looked as if he was just going to burst out laughing. He was dressed in a silken suit of light green, pink, pale yellow and sky blue, but all the colors were very much faded. On his head was stuck a tall orange-colored hat, with a lemon-colored feather.

"Is your father in?" said this strange personage.

"No, sir," said Loris. "He will be here this evening, and I can give him any message you may leave for him."

"I haven't any message," said the other. "I want to see him."

"You can see him about sun-set," said Loris, "if you will come then."

"I don't want to come again. I think I'll wait," said the man.

Loris said, "Very well," but she wondered what he would do all the afternoon. She brought out a stool for him to sit upon, for it was not very pleasant in the house, and there he sat for some

time looking at the chicken-house, where there were no chickens; and the cow-house, where there was no cow; and the pig-sty, where there were no pigs. Then he skipped up to the top of a little hillock near by and surveyed the landscape. Loris kept her eye upon him, to see that he did not go away without leaving a message, and went on with her cooking.

When her dinner was ready she thought it only right to ask him to have some. She did not want to do it, but she could not see how she could help it. She had been taught good manners. So she went to the door, and called him, and he instantly came skipping to her.

"I thought you might like to have some dinner, sir," she said. "I haven't much, but—"

"Two people don't want much," he said. "Where shall we have it? In the house, or will you spread the cloth out here on the grass?"

"There's not much use of spreading a cloth, sir," she said. "I have only one potato and some salt."

"That's not a dinner," said the other cheerfully. "A dinner is soup, meat, some vegetables (besides potatoes, and there ought to be two of them, at least), some bread, some cheese, pudding and fruit."

"But I haven't got all that, sir," said Loris, with her eyes wide open at this astonishing description of a dinner.

"Well, then, if you haven't got them the next best thing is to go and get them."

Loris smiled faintly. "I couldn't do that, sir," she said, "I have no money."

"Well, then, if you can't go the next best thing is for me to go. The village is not far away—just wait dinner a little while for me," and so saying he skipped away at a great pace.

Loris did not wait for him, but ate her potato and salt. "I'm glad he is able to buy his own dinner," she said, "but I'm afraid he won't come back. I wish he had left a message." But she need not have feared.

In a half-hour the queer man came back, bearing a great basket covered with a cloth. The latter he spread on the ground, and then set out all the things he had said were necessary to make up a dinner. He prepared a place at one end of the cloth for Loris, and one at the other end for himself.

"Sit down," said he, seating himself on the grass. "Don't let things get cold."

"I've had my dinner," said Loris. "This is yours."

"Whenever you're ready to begin," said the man, lying back on the grass and looking placidly up to the sky, "I'll begin. But not until then."

Loris saw he was in earnest, and, as she was a sensible girl, she sat down at the end of the cloth.

"That's right," gaily cried the queer man, sitting up again, "I was a little afraid you'd be obstinate and then I should have starved."

When the meal was over, Loris said, "I never had such a good dinner in my life."

The man looked at her and laughed. "This is a funny world, isn't it?" said he.

"Awfully funny!" replied Loris, laughing.

"You don't know what I am, do you?" said the man to Loris, as she gathered up the dishes and put them, with what was left of the meal, into the basket.

"No, sir; I do not," answered Loris.

"I am a Ninkum," said the other. "Did you ever meet with one before?"

"No, sir, never," said Loris.

200

"I am very glad to hear that," he said. "It's so pleasant to be fresh and novel." And then he went walking around the house again, looking at everything he had seen before. Soon he laid himself down on the grass, near the house, with one leg thrown over the other and his hands clasped under his head. For a long time he lay in this way, looking up at the sky and the clouds. Then he turned his head, and said to Loris, who was sewing by the door-step:

"Did you ever think how queer it would be if everything in the world were reversed; if the ground were soft and blue, like the sky, and if the sky were covered with dirt and chips and grass, and if fowls and animals walked about on it, like flies sticking to a ceiling?"

"I never thought of such a thing in my life," said Loris.

"I often do," said the Ninkum. "It expands the mind."

For the whole afternoon the Ninkum lay on his back, and expanded his mind, and then about sunset Loris saw her father returning. She ran to meet him, and told him of the Ninkum who was waiting to see him. Jorn hurried to the house, for he felt sure that his visitor must have an important job of work for him, as he had waited so long.

"I am glad you have come," said the Ninkum. "I wanted to see you very much, for two things. The first was that we might have supper. I'm dreadfully hungry, and I know there's enough in that basket for us all. The second thing can wait; it's business."

So Loris and the Ninkum spread out the remains of the dinner, and the three made a hearty supper. Jorn was highly pleased; he had expected to come home to a very different meal from this.

"Now, then," said the Ninkum, "we'll talk about the business."

"You have some work for me, I suppose," said Jorn.

"No," said the Ninkum, "none that I know of. What I want is for you to go into partnership with me."

"Partnership!" cried Jorn. "I don't understand you. What kind of work could we do together?"

"None at all," said the Ninkum, "for I never work. Your part of the partnership will be to chop wood, and mine, and plow, and do just what you do now. I will live here with you, and will provide the food, and the clothes, and the fuel, and the pocket-money for the three of us."

"But you couldn't live here," cried Loris, "our house is so poor, and there is no room for you."

"There need be no trouble about that," said the Ninkum. "I

can build a room, right here, on this side of the house. I never work," he said to Jorn, "but I hate idleness. So what I want is to go into partnership with a person who will work—an industrious person like you. Then my conscience will be at ease. Please agree as quickly as you can, for it's beginning to grow dark, and I hate to walk in the dark."

Jorn did not hesitate. He agreed instantly to go into partnership with the Ninkum, and the latter, after bidding them goodnight, skipped gaily away.

The next day, he returned with carpenters, and laborers, and lumber, and timber and furniture, and bedding, and a large and handsome room was built for him, on one side of the house, and he came to live with Jorn and Loris. For several days he had workmen putting a fence around the yard, and building a new cow-house, a new chicken-house, and a new pig-sty. He bought a cow, pigs and chickens, had flowers planted in front of the house, and made everything look very neat and pretty.

"Now," said he one day to Loris and Jorn as they were eating supper together, "I'll tell you something, I was told to keep it a secret, but I hate secrets; I think they all ought to be told as soon as possible. Ever so much trouble has been made by secrets.

The one I have is this: That dwarf, who came here, and then went and hired old Laub to work in his mine—"

"Was that a dwarf?" asked Loris, much excited.

"Yes, indeed," said the Ninkum, "a regular one. Didn't you notice how short he was? Well, he told me all about his coming here. The dwarfs in the Ragged Mine found a deep hole, with lots of gold at the bottom of it, but it steamed and smoked and was too hot for dwarfs. So the king dwarf sent out the one you saw, and told him to hire the first miner he could find, to work in the deep hole, but not to tell him how hot it was until he had made his contract. So the dwarf had to come first for you, Jorn, for you lived nearest the mine, but he hoped he would not find you, for he knew you were a good man. That was the reason he just gave one knock, and hurried on to Laub's house. And then he told me how Loris ran after him, and how good she was to agree to let him give the work to Laub, when she thought he needed it more than her father. 'Now,' says he to me, 'I want to do something for that family, and I don't know anything better that could happen to a man like Jorn than to go into partnership with a Ninkum.'"

At these words, Jorn looked over the well-spread supper-table, and he thought the dwarf was certainly right.

"So that's the way I came to live here," said the Ninkum, "and I like it first-rate."

"I wish I could go and see the dwarfs working in their mines," said Loris.

"I'll take you," exclaimed the Ninkum. "It's not a long walk from here. We can go tomorrow."

Jorn gave his consent, and the next morning Loris and the Ninkum set out for the Ragged Mine. The entrance was a great jagged hole in the side of a mountain, and the inside of the mine had also a very rough and torn appearance. It belonged to a colony of dwarfs, and ordinary mortals seldom visited it, but the Ninkum had no difficulty in obtaining admission. Making their way slowly along the rough and somber tunnel, Loris and he saw numbers of dwarfs, working with pick and shovel, in search of precious minerals.

Soon they met the dwarf who had come to Jorn's house, and he seemed glad to see Loris again. He led her about to various parts of the mine, and showed her the heaps of gold and silver and precious stones, which had been dug out of the rocks around them.

The Ninkum had seen these things before, and so he thought he would go and look for the hot hole, where Laub was working; that would be a novelty.

He soon found the hole, and just as he reached it, Laub appeared at its opening, slowly climbing up a ladder.

He looked very warm and tired, and throwing some gold ore upon the ground, from a basket which he carried on his back, he sat down and wiped the perspiration from his forehead.

"That is warm work, Laub," said the Ninkum, pleasantly.

"Warm!" said Laub, gruffly, "hot—hot as fire. Why, the gold down at the bottom of that hole burns your fingers when you pick it up. If I hadn't made a contract with these rascally dwarfs to work here for forty-one days, I wouldn't stay here another minute, but you can't break a contract you make with dwarfs."

"It's a pretty hard thing to have to work here, that is true," said the Ninkum, "but you owe your ill-fortune to yourself. It's all because you're known to be so ill-natured and wicked. When the dwarf was sent to hire a man to come and work in this hole, he had to go to Jorn's house first because that was the nearest place, but he just gave one knock there, and hurried away, hoping he didn't hear, for it would be a pity to have a good man like

Jorn working in a place like this. Then he went after you, for he knew you deserved to be punished by this kind of work."

As the Ninkum said this, Laub's face grew black with rage.

"So that's the truth!" he cried. "When I get out of this place, I'll crush every bone in the body of that sneaking Jorn," and, so saying, he rushed down into the hot hole.

"Perhaps I ought not to have told him all that," said the Ninkum, as he walked away, "but I hate secrets, they always make mischief."

When he joined Loris, the little girl said, "Let us go out of this place now. I have seen nearly everything, and it is so dark and gloomy."

Taking leave of the kind dwarf, the two made their way out of the mine.

"I do not like such gloomy places any better than you do," said the Ninkum. "Disagreeable things are always happening in them. I like to have things bright and lively. I'll tell you what would be splendid! To make a visit to the Castle of Bim."

"What is that, and where is it?" asked Loris.

"It's the most delightful place in the whole world," said the Ninkum. "While you're there you do nothing and see nothing but what is positively charming, and everybody is just as happy and gay as can be. It's all life and laughter, and perfect delight. I know you would be overjoyed if you were there."

"I should like very much to go," said Loris, "if father would let me."

"I'll go and ask him this minute," said the Ninkum. "I know where he is working. You can run home, and I will go to him, and then come and tell you what he says."

So Loris ran home, and the Ninkum went to the place where Jorn was cutting wood. "Jorn," said the Ninkum, "suppose that every thing in the world were reversed; that you chopped wood, standing on your head, and that you split your ax, instead of the log you struck. Would not that be peculiar?"

"Such things could not be," said Jorn. "What is the good of talking about them?"

"I think a great deal about such matters," said the Ninkum. "They expand my mind, and now, Jorn, reversibly speaking, will you let Loris go with me to the Castle of Bim?"

"Where is that?" asked Jorn.

"It is not far from here. I think we could go in half a day. I would get a horse in the village."

"And how long would you stay?"

"Well, I don't know. A week or two, perhaps. Come, now, Jorn, reversibly speaking, may she go?"

"No, indeed," said Jorn, "on no account shall she go. I could not spare her."

"All right," said the Ninkum. "I will not keep you from your work any longer. Good-morning."

As soon as he was out of Jorn's sight, the Ninkum began to run home as fast as he could.

"Get ready, Loris," he cried, when he reached the house. "Your father says, reversibly speaking, that on every account you must go. He can well spare you."

"But must we go now?" said Loris. "Cannot we wait until he comes home, and go tomorrow?"

"No, indeed," said the Ninkum. "There will be obstacles to our starting tomorrow. So let us hasten to the village, and hire a horse. Your father will get along nicely here by himself, and he will be greatly pleased with your improvement when you return from the Castle of Bim."

So Loris, who was really much pleased with the idea of the journey, hastened to get ready, and having put the house-key under the front door-stone, she and the Ninkum went to the village, where they got a horse and started for the Castle of Bim.

The Ninkum rode in front, Loris sat on a pillow behind, and the horse trotted along gaily. The Ninkum was in high good spirits, and passed the time in telling Loris of all the delightful things she would see in the Castle of Bim.

Late in the afternoon, they came in sight of a vast castle, which rose up at the side of the road like a little mountain.

"Hurrah!" cried the Ninkum, as he spurred the horse. "I knew we were nearly there!"

Loris was very glad that they had reached the castle, for she was getting tired of riding, and when the Ninkum drew up in front of the great portals, she felt sure that she was going to see wonderful things, for the door, to begin with, was, she felt sure, the biggest door in the whole world.

"You need not get off," said the porter, who stood by the door, to the Ninkum, who was preparing to dismount, "you can ride right in."

Accordingly, the Ninkum and Loris rode right in to the castle through the front door. Inside, they found themselves in a high and wide hall-way paved with stone, which led back to what appeared to be an inner court. Riding to the end of this hall, they stopped in the doorway there and looked out. In the center of the court, which was very large, there stood side by side, and about twenty feet apart, two great upright posts, like the trunks of tall pine trees. Across these, near their tops, rested a thick and heavy horizontal pole, and on this pole a giant was practicing gymnastics.

Hanging by his hands, he would draw himself up until his chin touched the pole. And again and again he did this, until the Ninkum said in a whisper, "Twelve times. I did not think he could do it."

The giant now drew up his legs and threw them over the bar above his head. Then, by a vigorous effort, he turned himself entirely over the bar, and hung beneath it by his hands. After stopping a minute or two to breathe, he drew up his legs again, and putting them under the bar, between his hands as boys do when they "skin the cat," he turned partly over, and hung in this position.

His face was now turned toward the doorway, and he first noticed his visitors.

"Hello!" said he to the Ninkum. "Could you do that?"

"Not on that pole," answered the Ninkum, smiling.

"I should think not," said the giant, dropping to his feet, and puffing a little. "Ten years ago, when I did not weigh so much, I could draw myself up twenty-seven times. Come in with me and have some supper. Is that your little daughter?"

"No," said the Ninkum, "I am her guardian for the present."

"Ride right up-stairs," said the giant. "My wife is up there and she will take care of the little girl."

"I am afraid," said the Ninkum, "that my horse cannot jump up those great steps."

"Of course not," said the giant. "Let me help you up, and then I will go down and bring your horse."

"Oh, that won't be necessary," said the Ninkum, and Loris laughed at the idea.

"You may want to look at the house," said the giant, "and then you will need your horse."

"So the giant took the Ninkum and Loris up-stairs, and then came down and brought up the horse. The upper story was as vast and spacious as the lower part of the castle, and by a window the giant's wife sat darning a stocking.

As they approached her, the Ninkum whispered to Loris: "If

there were such holes in my stockings I should fall through." The giantess was very glad to see Loris, and she took her up in her hand, and kissed her, very much as a little girl would kiss a canary bird. Then the giant children were sent for—two big boys and a baby girl, who thought Loris was so lovely that she would have squeezed her to death, if her mother had allowed her to take the little visitor in her hands.

During supper, Loris and the Ninkum sat in chairs with long legs, like stilts, which the giant had had made for his men and women visitors. They had to be very careful, lest they should tip over and break their necks.

After supper, they sat in the great upper hall, and the giant got up his guitar and sang them a song.

"I hope there are not many more verses," whispered the Ninkum to Loris. "My bones are almost shaken apart."

"How did you like that?" asked the giant, when he had finished.

"It was very nice," said the Ninkum; "it reminded me of something I once heard before—I think it was a wagon-load of copper pots rolling down a mountain, but I am not sure."

The giant thanked him, and soon after, they all went to bed.

213

Loris slept in the room with the giantess, on a high shelf where the children could not reach her.

Just before they went to their rooms the Ninkum said to Loris:

"Do you know that I don't believe this is the Castle of Bim?"

"It didn't seem to be like the place you told me about," said Loris, "but what are we to do?"

"Nothing, but to go to bed," said the Ninkum. "They are very glad to see us, and tomorrow we will bid them good-by, and push on to the Castle of Bim."

With this, the Ninkum jumped on his horse, and rode to his room.

The next day, after they had gone over the castle and seen all its sights, the Ninkum told the giant that he and Loris must pursue their journey to the Castle of Bim.

"What is that?" said the giant, and when the Ninkum proceeded to describe it to him, he became very much interested.

"Ho! Ho! good wife!" he cried. "Suppose we go with these friends to the Castle of Bim. It must be a very pleasant place, and the exercise will do me good. I'm dreadfully tired of gymnastics. What do you say? We can take the children."

The giantess thought it would be a capital idea, and so they all put on their hats and caps, and started off, leaving the castle in charge of the giants' servants, who were people of common size.

They journeyed all that day, Loris and the Ninkum riding ahead, followed by the giant, then by the giantess carrying the baby, and lastly the two giant boys with a basket of provisions between them.

That night they slept on the ground, under some trees, and the Ninkum admitted that the Castle of Bim was a good deal farther off than he had supposed it to be.

Toward afternoon of the next day they found themselves on some high land, and coming to the edge of a bluff, they saw, in the plain below, a beautiful city. The giant was struck with admiration.

"I have seen many a city," said he, "but I never saw one so sensibly and handsomely laid out as that. The people who built that place knew just what they wanted."

"Do you see that great building in the center of the city?" cried the Ninkum. "Well, that is the Castle of Bim. Let us hurry down." So, away they all started, at their best speed, for the city.

They had scarcely reached one of the outer gates, when they

were met by a citizen on horseback, followed by two or three others on foot. The horseman greeted them kindly, and said that he had been sent to meet them. "We shall be very glad," he said to the Ninkum, "to have you and the little girl come into our city tonight, but if those giants were to enter, the people, especially the children, would throng the streets to see them, and many would unavoidably be trampled to death. There is a great show tent out here, where they can very comfortably pass the night, and tomorrow we will have the streets cleared, and the people kept within doors. Then these great visitors will be made welcome to walk in and view the city."

The giants agreed to this, and they were conducted to the tent, where they were made very comfortable, while the Ninkum and Loris were taken into the city, and lodged in the house of the citizen who had come to meet them.

The next day the giants entered the city, and the windows and doors in the streets which they passed through were crowded with spectators.

The giant liked the city better and better, as he walked through it. Everything was so admirably pleasing, and in such perfect order. The others enjoyed themselves very much, too, and Loris was old enough to understand the beauty and conveniences of the things she saw around her.

Towards the end of the day, the Ninkum came to her.

"Do you know," said he, "that the Castle of Bim is not here? That large building is used by the governors of the city. And what a queer place it is! Everything that they do turns out just right. I saw a man set a rat-trap and what do you think? He caught the rat! I could not help laughing. It is very funny."

"But what are you going to do?" asked Loris.

"We will stay here tonight," said the Ninkum, "they are very kind—and tomorrow we will go on to the Castle of Bim."

The next day, therefore, our party again set out on their journey. The Ninkum had told the citizen, who had entertained him, where they were going and his accounts of the wonderful castle induced this worthy man to go with him.

"In our city," said he, "we try to be governed in everything by the ordinary rules of common sense. In this way we get along very comfortably and pleasantly, and everything seems to go well with us. But we are always willing to examine into the merits of things which are new to us, and so I would like to go to this curious castle, and come back and report what I have seen to my fellow-citizens."

His company was gladly accepted, and all set out in high good humor, the citizen riding by the side of Loris and the Ninkum.

But when they had gone several miles, the giantess declared that she believed she would go back home. The baby was getting very heavy, and the boys were tired. The giant could tell her about the Castle of Bim when he came home.

So the giantess turned back with her children, her husband kissing her good-by, and assuring her that he would not let her go back by herself if he did not feel certain that no one would molest her on the way.

The rest of the party now went on at a good pace, the giant striding along as fast as the horses could trot. The Ninkum did not seem to know the way as well as he had said he did. He continually desired to turn to the right, and, when the others inquired if he was sure that he ought to do this, he said that the best thing a person could do when a little in doubt was to turn to the right.

The citizen did not like this method of reasoning, and he was about to make an objection to it when a man was perceived sitting, in doleful plight, by the side of the road. The Ninkum who was very kind-hearted, rode up to him, to inquire what had happened to him, but the moment the man raised his head, and before he had time to say a word, Loris slipped off her horse and threw her arms around his neck.

"Oh, father! father!" she cried. "How came you here?"

It was indeed Jorn, ragged, wounded and exhausted.

In a moment everyone set to work to relieve him. Loris ran for water and bathed his face and hands; the citizen gave him some wine from a flask; the giant produced some great pieces of bread and meat; and the Ninkum asked him questions.

Jorn soon felt refreshed and strengthened, and then he told his story. He had been greatly troubled, when he found that Loris had gone away against his express orders.

"Why, father," cried Loris, at this point, "you said I could go."

"Never," said Jorn. "I said you could not go."

"Reversibly speaking," said the Ninkum, smiling, "he consented, that was the way I put the question to him. If I had not put it in that way, I should have told a lie."

Everybody looked severely at the Ninkum, and Loris was very angry, but her father patted her on the head, and went on with his story. He would have followed the Ninkum and his daughter, but he did not know what road they had taken, and as they were on a horse he could not, in any case, expect to catch up with them.

So he waited, hoping they would soon return, but, before long he was very glad that Loris was away.

The wicked Laub, who, in some manner, had found out that he had been made to work in the dwarfs' mine instead of Jorn, who had been considered too good for such disagreeable labor, had become so enraged that he broke his contract with the dwarfs, and, instead of continuing his work in the mine, had collected a few of his depraved companions, and had made an attack upon Jorn's house.

The doors had been forced, poor Jorn had been dragged forth, beaten, and forced to fly, while Laub and his companions took possession of the house and everything in it.

"But how could you wander so far, dear father?" asked Loris.

"It is not far," said Jorn; "our home is not many miles away."

"Then you have been going in a circle," said the citizen to the Ninkum, "and you are now very near the point you started from."

"That seems to be the case," said the Ninkum, smiling.

"But we won't talk about it now," said the citizen. "We must see what we can do for this poor man. He must have his house again."

"I would have asked the dwarfs to help me," said Jorn, "but I believe they would have killed Laub and the others if they had resisted, and I didn't want any blood shed."

"No," said the citizen. "I think we can manage it better than that. Our large friend here will be able to get these people out of your house without killing them."

"Oh, yes," said the giant, "I'll attend to that."

Jorn being now quite ready to travel, the party proceeded, and soon reached his house.

When Laub perceived the approach of Jorn and his friends, he barricaded all the doors and windows, and, with his companions, prepared to resist all attempts to enter.

But his efforts were useless. The giant knelt down before the house, and having easily removed the door, he thrust in his arm, and sweeping it around the room, easily caught three of the invaders.

He then put his other arm through the window of Ninkum's room, and soon pulled out Laub, taking no notice of his kicks and blows.

The giant then tied the four rascals in a bunch by the feet, and laid them on the grass.

"Now," said the citizen to the Ninkum, "as there seems to be nothing more to be done for this good man and his daughter, suppose you tell me the way to the Castle of Bim. I think I can find it, if I have good directions, and I do not wish to waste any more time."

"I do not know the exact way," answered the Ninkum.

"What!" cried the other. "Have you never been there?"

"No," said the Ninkum.

"Well, then, did not the person who told you about it tell you the way?"

"No one ever told me about it," replied the Ninkum. "I have thought a great deal on the subject, and I feel sure that there must be such a place, and the way to find it is to go and look for it."

"Well," said the citizen, smiling, "you are a true Ninkum. I suppose we have all thought of some place where everything shall be just as we want it to be, but I don't believe any of us will find that place. I am going home."

"And I too," said the giant, "and on my way I will stop at the Ragged Mine, and leave these fellows to the care of the dwarfs. They will see that they molest honest men no more."

"And I think I will go too," said the Ninkum. "I liked this place very much, but I am getting tired of it now."

"That will be a good thing for you to do," said the citizen, who had heard the story of how the Ninkum had been sent to Jorn and Loris, as a reward. "You have lived for a time with these good people, and have been of some service to them, but I am quite sure they now feel that partnership with a Ninkum is a very dangerous thing, and should not be kept up too long."

"No doubt that's true," said the Ninkum. "Good-by, my friends. I will give you my room and everything that is in it."

"You have been very kind to us," said Loris.

"Yes," said Jorn, "and you got me work that will last a long time."

"I did what I could," cried the Ninkum, mounting his horse, and gaily waving his hat around his head, "and, reversibly speaking, I took you to the Castle of Bim."

SLIMME SIR MARMADUKE

by Henry Groff Dodge

A doughty knyght was Marmaduke,
   A doughty knyght, but slimme—
So slimme, forsooth, that no fence-rayle
   Could be compared to hym.
"Sir Marmaduke de Launcelot
   Gahalapeter Jones"—
Such was ye noble nayme he bore;
   Hys crest, ye skull and bones.

But Marmaduke, despyte hys wydth,
   Was valorous and bolde,
And when he put hys stove-pypes on
   Was fearsome to beholde.
He'd slayn full twentie dragons, in
   Ye regulation way,
And rescuing a princess was
   For hym ye merest play.

One summer's day he sallyde forth
   Upon hys trustie nagge,
To finde some awful monster
   Or some dragon he myght bagge.
He journeyed far, he journeyed long,
   No dragon mette hys syght;
He traveled all ye livelong day,
   Unto ye very nyght.

But when ye day was nearly donne
   He saw, to hys dismay,
A giant with a sturdie clubbe
   A-coming down ye way.
Full twentie cubits was hys hyght,
   Hys legges were lyke to trees,
Hys massive arms with hairy fystes
   Hung nearly to hys knees.

He spyed ye warrior from afar,
   And bellowed as he ranne;
And sure he was a horryd syght,
   To fryghten any manne.
Sir Marmaduke, erstwhile so brave,
   Was like to die of fear;
He thought hys syze would serve hym welle,
   And hidde behynd hys spear.

Ye giant then was sore perplexed,—
   He hadde not seen hym hyde,—
And would have gone hadde not Jones' ears
   Stuck out on either side.

He ranne around and caught hym there,
   And hadde hym soon fast bounde,
And started home, a-draggyng Jones
   Behynd along ye ground.

Ere long they reached ye giant's hold,
    And Marmaduke was cast
Into a darksome coal-cellar.
    Ye door was bolted fast.
He slypped hys chayns and looked about—
    Hys celle was colde and bare.
But suddenly he hearde a steppe
    A-coming down the staire.

In fryght he shrank agaynst ye walle;
    Ye door was opened wyde,
And then a buxom giantess
    Stepped jauntily insyde.
"Where are my tongs?" quoth she, aloude.
    And Marmaduke perceived
That she knew not that he was there,
    And strayghtway felte relieved.

Now Marmaduke, we should have sayd,
    Was all encased in steel,
And wyth hys longe and slender legges
    Would look, and even feel,

To giant's eyes, just lyke a pair
   Of tongs with knobbie head,
And so the Madame, groping rounde,
   Found Marmaduke instead.

At first poor Jones was terror-strook,
   But quyckly he took hearte,
And, synce she'd taken him for tongs,
   Resolved to acte hys parte.

And so when she had seized hys legges,
  And thrust them in ye binne,
He caught a piece between hys feet,
  And then hung on lyke synne.

She fetched hym up ye wyndyng stayr
  Into ye room above,
Then deftlie stretched hys legges and dropped
  Ye coal into ye stove.
Then, luckyly for Marmaduke,
  She didde not take hym back,
But stood hym in ye corner,
  In a handie little rack.

A moment, and she left the room
  To calle her husbande, maybe,
Mayhap to go and rock to sleep
  Ye lyttle giant baby.
(In any case our Marmaduke
  Soon hearde ye baby's roars.)
No sooner was she out of syght
  Than he was out of doors.

He crept around ye castle walles
  Upon hys handes and knees,
And found hys nagge besyde ye gate,
  A-nybblyng at her ease.
"That tyme," quoth he, as home he rode,
  "My leanness served me welle.
And how surprysed Hys Nybbs will be
  To see my emptie celle!"

THE TWO LITTLE MEN

by Malcolm Douglas

There were two little men of ye olden tyme
   Of their manners so very proud
That each would try to outdo in grace
   The other, whene'er they bowed.
They would bend, and bend, and bend so low
   That finally, it was said,
Their three-cornered hats would touch the ground.
   And then each stood on his head!

233

GEORGE O'GREEN AND ROBIN HOOD
by Caroline Brown

GEORGE O'GREEN AND ROBIN HOOD

IN THE dusky aisles of the greenwood caroled lustily a man, clad in Lincoln green from top to toe, as he took his way blithely adown the woodland path:

> "Oh, give me my bent bow of yew;
> Oh, give me my lads so good and true;
> Oh, give me my forest so wild and green,
> And the dappled deer the boles between!"

"I must take me further afield if I would have adventure this day," he mused, thinking aloud. " 'Tis but five o' the clock, and a good ten miles from Nottingham. It may happen a fat monk will pass, with purse well filled with gold." Thrusting his hand into his pocket he drew it out empty, and looked at it with rueful countenance. "But alack! mine is as empty as yon nest!" —glancing at a wood-pigeon's nest atop a sturdy oak. " 'Twould be a fine frolic to fill it from some fat purse in the priory yonder."

A few steps brought him to a cool dell wherein bubbled a

brown spring, now somber in the deep shadows, but under the sun rays sparkling as a crystal cup. He stooped, and drank a draught from its depths, and again proceeded on his way to the outskirts of the forest where ran the road. When he came in sight of it, he saw, slowly coming toward him, two lean monks, whose habits were gray with dust of the highway. Their cheeks were sunken with fasting, and their steps slow and uncertain.

The man in green hid behind a tree, and laughed softly, as he said:

"If any purse they have, 'tis empty! The mendicant friars ne'er carry coin in their purse, nor victual in their wallet."

The monks dragged wearily out of sight, with slow and solemn gait. When they were well away he took to the road, and set off down Nottingham way. He walked for a matter of two miles, when he came to a glebe parceled out to the country folk thereabout for pasture. There he found, stretched out at full length, on a bank of thyme bordering a brook, a young country fellow of great breadth and brawn, fast asleep, although it was now full day. As he approached, a lark rose high in spiral curve till it seemed lost in the ribbon-like clouds that streaked the blue sky, then trilled forth a song so sweet and joyous to greet the day,

that the forester raised his cap in reverence.

"Aha, bonny bird! Hast borrowed an angel's song? And yet that lout sleeps!" So saying he prodded the churl with the oaken staff till he grunted like one of the pigs that strayed near.

"Sandy, thou varlet!" the sleeper muttered drowsily; "is't 'ee again?" and he raised his great bulk half up, supporting it on his elbow, as he rubbed his eyes free of sleep.

"And who may Sandy be?" put in a blithe, laughing voice.

"Sandy is the canniest pig i' all the country-side," said the man, fully rising. "Aye, that pig, there's naa lout i' a' the parish that's wiser than he be!"

"Hoot, toot, man!" quoth Robin Hood—for the man in green with the laughing voice was he—"how canst thou make such speech! Thou knowest *me* not!"

The man standing on his feet towered over Robin two or three inches, a very giant in girth and stature. His face betokened dullness and good nature.

"Na-a, by the good Saint Dunstan I know thee not," he said; "but I know my pigs. There's the speckled pig, that's the slyest beast o' the lot; and the red pig—that's Sandy—he has a coat like a borderman's poll, so I calls him by that name—he's uncommon wise; and there's the black—"

"That'll do, man! Pigs are pigs till they be killed, then they be bacon! But tell me how a man o' the brawn and bone o' thee comes to be minding pigs? Why, man, any bairn could do as much!"

The man muttered, "They're none o' mine. They be Goody Hoskins's, an' she gi'es me a sixpence, and a bed at night, and a bowl o' porridge morn and eve, and an oatcake at noontide for mindin' 'em."

"So, thou'rt a pig-minder when thou mightest be the greatest wrestler hereabout, or even carry a free lance!"

"Eh? Think'st thou so?" said the man stupidly. "But I couldn't sleep between mindin' as I can now. When the pigs stray too far afield Sandy cooms and grunts to warn me. Then I take my withe and beat 'em back to our part of the glebe. And so I make shift to live."

"Now, I doubt me if in all that brawn there lurk one ounce of strength," muttered Robin. "How art thou called, Master Pig-minder?"

"George O'Green."

"Why that?"

"Ho, ho, ho!" roared the churl. "So wise, and don't know that withal! Why, I live on the green and mind the pigs!" And he wiped tears of laughter from his eyes on the sleeve of his fustian jerkin.

"I doubt me," said Robin, "if thou canst play with the quarter-staff."

"Aye, but I can!" said George, quickly.

"Show thy prowess then!" said Robin, with a quick thrust at him with his white-oak staff.

"Bide here and mind the pigs till I go to yon thicket and get me a staff."

Robin consented, and gazed after the brawny man as he walked with long, slow strides to the oak thicket on the hither side of the brook. There he carefully selected a tough green sapling, almost two inches thick, and then wrenched it off near the ground with a twist of his powerful hands.

"This bodes me no good in the coming tilt," thought Robin. But though he never withdrew for any cause, rarely had he suffered defeat.

George turned him about, and, coming up to Robin, said:

"Canst lend me that knife o' thine? 'Tis o'er too frayed for a good staff," he said, looking at the fringe of splinters where he had snapped off the stem.

He trimmed the staff carefully, then handed back to Robin his knife. But chancing to look around, he saw the pigs scampering off to a distant corner of the common.

"Thou'st not minded the pigs! Now Goody Hoskins will rate me well!" cried George with heat, yet timidly withal.

"But Sandy didn't give *me* warning!" pleaded Robin.

"Good old Sandy! Faithful shoat! He knows thee not. He'll talk only to me!" and George's ill-nature left him at this proof of the faithfulness of his favorite.

He set off at full speed after the pigs, Robin at his heels. When they had got the swine back to their own feeding-ground they laid themselves down on the short thymy turf to rest. The chase had been a right merry one, and both were short of wind; for the pigs had scampered and dodged sprightfully in a way that made the men more weary than a five-mile sprint.

George dozed off on the instant, and Robin panted loud. In ten minutes Robin prodded George with his staff, and said:

"Sluggard! Art ready?"

George yawned prodigiously, showing strong teeth, white as

a young dog's, rimming his jaws. Then he rose and ran his fingers through his shock of red hair, stretched mightily, and said briefly:

"I be. Lay on!"

"Well, then," cried Robin, "stand forth now and defend thyself! I'll warrant thou wilt be no longer sleepy when I shall have done with thee!"

At once the sound of the clashing of staves filled the air. As both were so deft in handling the staff, all blows were skillfully parried. At the end of an hour Robin's arm began to weary, but George's brawny arm was unfailing. In warding off a powerful blow Robin's arm swerved, and George's staff came down on his crown with a sharp rap, the first hit made by either. For near two hours longer the clashing of staves kept up, when Robin's foot slipped on the thyme, and down he rolled into the brook.

George greeted his fall with hoarse guffaws, bending double and clinging to his staff to keep from falling, so tickled was he at Robin's sorry plight. Robin climbed out of the brook spluttering and gasping, and gave himself a mighty shake, which sent the water flying in a shower all about him.

When George could speak for laughing he said:

"Rest thee here and let the sun dry 'ee a bit while I gather the pigs."

The beasts had again strayed, led by the treacherous Sandy, who like a bad boy took advantage of his master's unheeding.

George set off in a shambling run, and Robin threw himself down full length on the ground. Soon George came back with all his pigs; but Sandy was not in favor this time, and George took his oaken staff, and laid it lustily over the pig's back till he squealed loud and shrill.

"Take that for thy pay, base varlet that thou art!" said George, as seriously as if the red pig were a naughty boy. "Hast not eaten of my porridge, and shared my oaten cake? I'll not favor thee next time!"

For reply Sandy grunted "Ugh, ugh, ugh!" as he rubbed his smarting back against a low shrub.

Glancing up at the sky, where hung the sun in the middle, George exclaimed:

"The morn hath passed right merrily. It is noontide. Wilt share my oaten cake?"

And he drew it from the pocket of his jerkin and broke it in

246

two.

"Right gladly," said Robin, "for such a morning's bout whetteth one's appetite."

They sat them down on the bank, and each munched his cake in silence, and washed it down by a draught of water from the brook out of a cup made of a dock-leaf.

"Hast had enough?" queried George of Robin, whose nether garments were still steaming in the sun's heat.

"Not I," quoth Robin; "nor till one or t'other hath proven the better man. And I bethink me, George O'Green, thou'rt a better man than first I thought thee." This last Robin said to himself.

They set to again. This time both were in earnest, each eager to prove himself the victor, and the blows fell thick and fast on pates and shoulders. Many a hard rap George gave, and many a skillful blow Robin dealt; for the advantage George had in strength Robin made up in skill.

The pigs were again forgot, and had long since routed Farmer Arkell's swine from their allotted corner of the glebe, and were enjoying the forbidden ground as only pigs or vagrants could.

The sun began to decline, and still the staves clashed, not so briskly and merrily, but warily and carefully. Each blow was studied. Five hours they had been at it since the nooning, and the graying light betokened but a few hours of day.

Robin heaved a mighty sigh, for he was well-nigh spent, and, raising his hand to his head to dash off drops of sweat that were trickling into his eyes, his staff fell with a feeble blow against George's, while the pig-minder's sapling came down on Robin's head with a crash that laid him low and well-nigh brained him. For a moment he lay stunned. George ran to the brook, and, gathering water into the bowl made of his two hands, dashed it into Robin's face.

Robin came to himself, and rose up on his elbow. Said George to his fallen foe:

"Hast had enough?"

"Look I not like a man that knows when he hath enough?" said Robin, testily. Then rising to his feet, he took George by the hand and said:

"Thou'rt the first to lay Robin Hood low."

George's chin fell, and his eyes stuck out; for until that moment he had not known the name of his friendly foe.

"I—I—knew thee not!" he stammered, "or by St. Dunstan—"

and he choked so he could say no more.

"Nay, nay!" said Robin, good-naturedly. "Take it not so. Thou'rt too good a man to mind pigs. Come! Go with me to Sherwood, and I'll give thee occupation worthy of thy brawn and bone."

"But Goody Hoskins—and the pigs—and Sandy—" faltered George.

"I'll have speech with the good dame, or my gold will speak for me"—thrusting his hand in his pocket. He drew it out empty, while a rueful look spread over his face. "Never mind, 'twill soon fill again. Wilt go with me if I can win thee from the good dame?"

George trembled and whimpered. "The good dame, as thou call'st her, hath a bitter tongue. She'll rate thee up hill and down dale."

Robin laughed, then his lip curled with scorn.

"I've ne'er seen matron or maid but I could win a smile from by soft words. Enough. Courage! And let's set off to Goody Hoskins's cot."

They gathered the pigs and started, each man using his staff, that but now had played so merrily about the other's crown, to keep the drove together. Betimes they reached the hovel of Goody Hoskins. It was made of sticks and stones plastered together with mud, and the roof was of thatch, with a hole in the middle for the smoke to go out. The dame was busy, bending over a little fire, stirring porridge with a long wooden ladle, for her supper. When the squeal of the pigs broke on her ear, she rose hastily, and a flush of anger spread over her face. She hobbled to the door, and cried out:

"Thou lazy varlet! Late again! Only half a porringer shall be thy portion tonight!"

Robin looked surprised at George—who stood the picture of fear, twisting his fingers and shuffling his feet, but saying not a word—and wondered if he could be the same man that had used his staff so lustily and valiantly against him. Now he seemed too much affrighted to speak.

Robin advanced and took off his cap. Bowing low, he said:

"Good mother, the blame rests with me. This man hath done me service that hath taken his time; but had I known it should have been devoted to thee, believe me, naught would have made me accept it. It hath ever been my delight to yield to such as thee!"

The old dame's looks softened, and she made answer:

"If he hath done aught for thee thou'rt right welcome; but 'tis little he does but eat and sleep and snore like one of his own pigs!" and she shook her crooked finger in George's face till his knees knocked together with fright.

"Is not the fellow faithful in his minding?"

"No, no; a younker of ten could do better!"

252

"Why not get rid of so worthless a churl, then?" said Robin, bending a look of contempt on George.

Stupid George looked surprised, and was about to protest when Robin gave him a glance that warned him to be silent and let Robin do the talking.

"Farmer Arkell's son Peter asked but today to mind my pigs along o' his, and he wants no bed nor porridge, only the six-pence."

"Then why not take him?"

"Why, I ha' na the sixpence that he must ha', he saith, every sennight."

"Those thou gavest George will do, I bethink me," said Robin.

"Oh," broke in the guileless George, "I ha' to gi'e 'em to Goody Hoskins to pay as fines to Farmer Arkell for letting my pigs stray into his part of the glebe. It's a ha'penny every time."

Robin bent a shrewd look on the old dame, and said:

"Ah, I see! If I send thee five shillings will that do, good mother, to pay the lad? I have it not about me now. But I'll send it thee!"

"Nor ever will!" snapped the old woman, suspicious at once.

"Good dame, didst ever hear of Robin Hood wronging any

woman?"

"I never did. But thou'rt not he. He goeth forth with three-score followers and his purse is always well lined!" said the old dame scornfully.

"Thou believest me not! I'll soon prove thee the truth!" and he drew from under his cloak a silver horn on which he blew three short blasts. After a little there was a crackling in the bushes at the right, and a splash in the brook, and a sound of rustling leaves, and lo!—about him there stood a score of men dressed in Lincoln green, all that were within sound of his magic horn. They now thronged closely to his side.

"What's your will, good master?" asked one, a youth who, under his mantle of green, was clad in scarlet from top to toe.

"Only that thou tell yon dame who I am."

"Thou'rt Robin Hood!" "A free archer of Sherwood forest." "And captain of a lusty band of rangers," came in chorus from the score of throats.

The old dame curtesied low, and said, nothing abashed:

"I e'en believe thou art he! Wilt share my porridge? Yon lout can have none. His share shall fall to thee."

Robin laughed and thanked her, but declined her courtesy.

"Hath any man of you five shillings?"

Twenty hands dived into twenty pockets, and all came out empty.

Each man stared at the other with blank looks.

"It's not so great a matter. 'Easy come, easy go!' Tomorrow, good dame, I'll pay thee thy shillings, and Jock O'Nimble Heels shall fetch them," said Robin, laying his hand on the shoulder of a stripling that stood near.

"Meantime take this as earnest of my faith," and he drew from his thumb a golden ring and pressed it in her palm.

"Now this lout may go with me?" pointing with his thumb over his shoulder at George, who had shrunk back at the rating tongue of the dame.

"Yes, yes; but forget not my silver," she said persistently.

George bent to Robin's ear and said, in a faltering whisper:

"But I canna go wi' thee. I canna leave Sandy."

"Sandy! Who might Sandy be?" asked Robin in surprise. "Ah!"—recollecting—"yon red shoat!" and he placed his hands on his hips and laughed long and loud. "Thou shalt take thy pet along," he said softly. "Leave it to me!"

"But he's not mine i' the law."

"Pooh, pooh, I'll make him thine!"

Turning to Dame Hoskins, he said:

"Good dame, canst spare a pig for six good bottles of sack? It seems to me 'twould taste right well, roasted whole."

A look of fear crossed George's face, and he was about to object when Robin trod on his toe and made him cry out, thus turning his attention, and interrupting his speech. The dame seemed bent on haggling, but soon consented to the bargain, and asked:

"Which wilt 'ee have?"

"Oh, any one! The easiest-caught!" said Robin, with a knowing wink at George, who at once chased off after the whole drove, and soon came back with Sandy squealing and squirming under his arm.

Robin's men all grinned at their master's cunning, and he himself hid the smile on his lips by stroking his mustache.

"To the forest, men! For the sun declines. The wood-dove even now sobs for his homing-mate, and the nightingale will soon sing from yonder copse."

They all set off smartly toward the forest, Robin and George, with Sandy under his arm, bringing up the rear. The men sang cheerily, accompanied by the squeals and grunts of Sandy:

> "Oh, give me my staff of whitest thorn;
> Oh, give me my bow of yew;
> Oh, give me the dun deer's dappled side;
> And my arrow stanch and true.
> Tirralee, tirrala, tirralee!
> There be none so happy, none so free,
> As the men that live under the Greenwood tree."

When at last they reached the forest, the moon, cut clean in the middle like half a warden pie, lit up but faintly the forest paths; but they made their way through them as readily as if the noontide sun himself filtered through the laced boughs of beech and oak over their heads, making a tunnel of greenery. The nightingale sang softly from its bower in a wild-rose, and from the top of an oak, near to the road, an owl suddenly called out its never-answered question, "Who, who?"

"Why, Robin Hood and his merry men," gaily answered Jock O'Nimble Heels.

"Hey, youngster, bandy not words with yon bird of night, for he can blight thee with his spell. 'Tis best to be friends with his ilk," said grim John O'Groats.

For a few moments there was silence. Twigs crackled underfoot, and forest sounds that had been all unnoticed made themselves heard, the falling of leaves and the stir of sleeping birds, the crickets' homely song, and the distant creak of frogs. A gleam of red flashed on their sight, and silence fled.

" 'Tis good Friar Tuck and Little John roasting the deer," said Will Scarlett.

And each man gave a joyous shout. A few moments brought them to the trysting tree, and into the full glare of the huge fire where the two men were busily roasting a deer for their suppers.

"Is the buck roasted to a turn?" queried Robin. "Hunger, they say, is a good sauce; and, by my troth, we bring our share to the feast this eve."

"Aye, aye; a minute's patience, and 'tis done," said Friar Tuck as he blew a breath coolingly upon the back of his hand, which had been for a moment too near the fire.

"But whom have we here?" he asked in surprise, as George's huge bulk was revealed in the leaping flame.

" 'Tis George O'Green, erstwhile a valiant pig-minder to as cross-grained an old dame as e'er stirred porridge." And Robin roared again as he thought of George's fear of Goody Hoskins, and the men joined in, as George gravely set down the grunting pig.

All eyes were bent on him, and he bore their looks but ill, shuffling his feet, and twisting his fingers, and keeping his bashful eyes turned toward the ground.

"Thou hast snared a brave bawcock, good Robin," sneered Little John.

Robin made answer, "He who hath a mind to beat a dog will easily find a stick. Wait till he hath supped and try him in a bout at wrestling, good Little John!"

"That I will; and now, if thou sayest so!"

"No; after," said Robin decisively. "We are both nigh famished —have only fed upon one oat-cake since morn."

At that moment Friar Tuck announced the buck was done to a turn, and all fell to. After they had eaten excellently, and had rested at full length on the sward for a space, Robin said:

"Now, good Little John, since thou art so eager, just try yon younker in a wrestling bout."

" 'Twere a pity to bruise so much brawn!" laughed Little John.

The two men took position, and at the fall of an oaken twig set to. The fire leaped high, and the half moon added her misty light to the strange scene. The men writhed and twisted, this way and that, till their breath came in gasps like those of hunted stags. Then all of a sudden Little John came sprawling at full length on the ground at Robin's feet, flung clean over George's shoulder.

" 'Twere ne'er done before!" panted Little John, ruefully.

"We must all have our fall, 'twould seem," quoth Robin, with a wise smile.

After George had rested a little Jock O'Nimble Heels said to him: "Well, good George O'Green, canst leap yon hazel clump i' the widest part?"

This was Jock's great feat, and at it he had ne'er been worsted. George only grinned, and nodded "yes."

Thereupon young Jock threw off his jerkin of leather, and running swiftly for four or five yards, cleared at a bound the thicket he had chosen; but as he descended his feet scraped the other side. A cheer greeted him, while the men nodded to each other as if to say, "He will ne'er beat that!"

George rose, shook back his red hair, bent toward the ground, swung his long arms to and fro, and in one tremendous bound his great bulk rose with the lightness of a bird, cleared the bush,

and landed full four feet beyond. There was no cheer to greet
him—only deep silence, for they were too surprised to speak.

Robin called him to his side and asked:

"Canst use the short cudgel?"

"A little, good master," answered George, modestly.

"Here, Friar Tuck, art thou willing to show this clown how
handy thou art i' the matter of short cudgels?"

Friar Tuck threw back his cowl, slipped off his sandals, and,
baring his brawny arm to the shoulder, cried "Come on!" as he
brandished his cudgel—a club of white thorn about three feet
long and thick as a man's arm.

"Hast no cudgel, George?" asked Robin. "Well, go to yonder
tree"—pointing to a little thorn growing near—"and pluck one."

The men all grinned, for they thought it but a pleasant jest of
Robin's. To their amaze, the man walked to the tree, chose a
branch, and broke it from the trunk as if 'twere an osier twig.
Friar Tuck threw down his cudgel.

"I can fight fist to fist with man, but not with the evil one,"
quoth he.

" 'Tis thy true work!" shouted the men together. They crowded
round George, and grasped his hand heartily in congratulation.

261

"Think you he's worthy to belong to the merry men o' Sherwood?" asked Robin.

"Aye, aye," came a chorus of answers.

"And, my men, there be something more. He hath this day beaten me and my good oak staff in a bout lasting from morn till nigh set of sun; but was himself worsted by the clattering, unruly little tongue in a woman's head."

A shout of laughter greeted this, and jests flew from mouth to mouth.

"Henceforth," said Robin, "let it be said, when one excels in anything, 'Thou'rt as good as George O'Green'; for he hath beaten each of us in what he does most excel."

And so it is to this day the proverb stands.

STAR-LIGHT

Star-light, star-bright,
First star I see tonight;
Wish I may, wish I might
Get the wish I wish tonight.

POLICEMAN'S SONG

from THE PIRATES OF PENZANCE

by W. S. Gilbert

When a felon's not engaged in his employment,
Or maturing his felonious little plans,
His capacity for innocent enjoyment
Is just as great as any honest man's.
Our feelings we with difficulty smother
When constabulary duty's to be done.
Ah, take one consideration with another,
A policeman's lot is not a happy one.

When the enterprising burglar's not a-burgling,
When the cut-throat isn't occupied in crime,
He loves to hear the little brook a-gurgling,
And listen to the merry village chime.
When the coster's finished jumping on his mother,
He loves to lie a-basking in the sun.
Ah, take one consideration with another,
The policeman's lot is not a happy one.

PRINCE CAM AND THE FAIRIES
by Sydney Reid

PRINCE CAM AND THE FAIRIES

IN A BEAUTIFUL valley in India lived little Prince Cam, who was beloved by all his people. He was an orphan, only twelve years of age, yet he ruled the valley and mountains as far as the eye could reach, and owned a thousand horses and five hundred elephants. Oranges, figs, dates, apples, pears, and other fine fruits grew in groves about his palace. He had more servants than he could count in a day, and seven rooms of the palace were filled with gold, silver, diamonds, rubies, pearls, emeralds, opals, topazes, and other beautiful gems, the very largest in the world.

But Prince Cam's Grand Vizir, Boorum Boola, had a bad heart, and envied the Prince.

Now the Grand Vizir's son, Suley, was just the Prince's age, and so like him that, when dressed alike, no one could tell them apart.

One day Suley said to his father, "Why can I not be prince? I am as tall as Cam." "We will see," said the Grand Vizir. He called two black slaves, and told them to seize Prince Cam when he slept, carry him to the forest, and leave him there clothed in rags.

The slaves did so, and the Grand Vizir put Suley in the Prince's bed. In the morning he made a great lamentation, declaring that Suley had been carried off in the night. The people were not sorry, for Suley was cruel and proud.

When Suley sat on the throne and the people brought their petitions, they found a great change. Prince Cam had always said "Yes," and smiled. Suley said "No," and frowned, and there was great sorrow and fear; for all said:

"The good little Prince has gone mad."

For a long time Prince Cam wandered about in the forest, becoming very hungry and tired. He met many people and told who he was, but they laughed and said:

"Little boy, you have been dreaming! Princes never dress in rags."

His misfortunes made him sad, but his heart was as kind as ever, and he was always gentle to every living creature.

One evening, just as the sun was setting, the poor young Prince came to a field of flowers. He stooped to pluck a large white lily, but as he grasped the stem, he saw a number of tiny men and

women dancing on the waxen floor of the lily bell. They were clothed in robes of rainbow and sunshine, and their king sat on a throne of pure gold, and wore a diamond dewdrop for a crown. A banquet-table was spread in front of the throne, and the dancers drank goblets of honey and dew.

Prince Cam drew back, but the king said:

"Why do you not take the flower?"

"I was unwilling to disturb you," said the Prince.

"What of that?" asked the king. "We are too small to fight one so big and strong as you."

"All the more reason why I should not harm you," said Prince Cam. "I would be glad to do you a service if I could; but I am poor and friendless now, though I was once rich and happy."

Now the fairies knew all about Prince Cam.

"Tell me your story," said the fairy king. So Prince Cam told how he had been seized in the night, carried to the woods, and left there clothed in rags.

"If you will take advice from a little person like me," said the fairy king, "go back to your kingdom, and ask the Grand Vizir to restore you to your throne. If he refuses, come and tell me. This road leads straight to your palace gate."

272

Prince Cam walked all night, and arrived before his palace gate in the morning. When he entered the court, Suley was sitting on the throne, surrounded by a band of wicked youths whom he had chosen to be his courtiers.

These made great sport of the dusty little beggar-boy.

"What is your petition?" they inquired; "—that the king should make you a great lord?"

"No. I have come to ask him to give me my kingdom back, for I am Prince Cam," was the reply.

All the courtiers laughed so loudly that the palace shook.

"What does the boy say?" asked the Grand Vizir.

"He says he is Prince Cam, and he wants his kingdom," said the courtiers.

The Grand Vizir and Suley laughed too.

"Come here, little boy," said the Vizir.

When Prince Cam approached him, the Vizir, who knew him well, said:

"Do you not see the Prince sitting on his throne?"

"I am Prince Cam, and he who sits on the throne is your son Suley," said the Prince.

"Tell that story to the tigers in the jungle," said the Vizir, with

273

a sneer. "If you can persuade one of them, I will believe it!"

The Vizir laughed again, but Suley frowned, and said to the slaves who had carried Cam away, "Turn the little beggar out; but first be sure that you warm his feet with a cane-fire so that he may walk well."

So Prince Cam was turned out and beaten on the feet with a cane, and he went back to the fairy sadder than he had come. But the fairy bade him be of good cheer. "Let us go and see what the tigers will say," said the fairy.

At this, one of the attendants led up a cricket, richly harnessed. The king sprang upon his back, and off went Prince Cam and the fairy, the king leading the way.

They traveled into the forest, and stopped at last under a great tree which had a hollow trunk. "Put your hand in the hollow, and see what you find," said the king.

Prince Cam pulled out an iron pot full of pitch and bird-lime.

"Sprinkle it all about on the leaves," said the king; and Prince Cam did so.

Then the king began to growl like a tiger who wanted to fight. Instantly a great tiger came running to see who had dared invade his dominions. When he beheld Prince Cam, he roared and lashed his sides.

"M-m-m, r-r-r-r-r!" said the fairy king, sitting on the cricket's back. The tiger thought it was Prince Cam who challenged him.

"M-m-m, r-r-r-r-r!" said the king, again.

The tiger lost all patience, and sprang at Prince Cam. The leaves stuck to his paws. More angry than ever, he jumped in the air and tried to scratch them off; but they stuck fast, and he gathered more of them all the time.

"Oh, what a coward!" said the fairy king. "Why don't you come on?"

That made the tiger furious. He rolled on the ground and gathered more leaves till he was nothing but a big, round ball. At length his eyes were covered, he could not see, and lay still.

"Promise me on your honor that you will obey all my instructions, and I will release you," said the king.

When the tiger had given the necessary pledge, Prince Cam brought some water and soon made him as sleek and clean as ever.

"You must acknowledge this youth as Prince," said the little king. "Now take him on your back."

Prince Cam mounted the tiger's back, and galloped swiftly to the palace, the king hopping along beside him on the cricket.

As they went down the road, the people all ran after them, for they had never seen a beggar-boy on a tiger before.

Prince Cam rode into the court and dismounted before the throne of the wicked Suley.

"I come to hold you to your promise," he said to the Grand Vizir.

Then turning to the tiger, Prince Cam said:

"Do you acknowledge me as the lawful ruler?"

276

The tiger bowed three times and touched his forehead to the ground.

"That is a trick," said Boorum Boola; "I can do that;" and he approached the tiger.

"Do you acknowledge me as the lawful ruler?" he asked.

The tiger rose on his hind legs and opened his mouth to swallow the Grand Vizir. But the Vizir jumped through the window and ran away in a great fright.

Suley trembled, but putting on a bold face, he asked the same question.

The tiger gave a terrible roar, and opened his mouth wider than ever. Suley jumped through the window, and ran after his father. He was just in time, for the tiger's teeth closed with a snap that could be heard far and wide; as it was, he tore off Suley's fine sash.

Then the people set up a great shout.

"Good Prince Cam has come again!" they said. So they seized the wicked and lazy courtiers, gave them a good beating, and packed them off to find the old Vizir and Suley, and ran to release Prince Cam's faithful servants and advisers.

Then they dressed the good Prince in the finest robes, and set

him on his throne.

"Reign forever!" they said; "for you are worthy."

And peace and plenty came again to the kingdom of good Prince Cam.

"So far, so good!" said the fairy king. "Now you want a wife. Would you not like to wed my daughter?"

"Is she not too small?" asked the Prince.

"You shall see," answered the king. He stamped his foot thrice, and the princess appeared.

Never had Prince Cam seen anyone so beautiful. Her dress was of the finest rose leaves looped up with dewdrops, her long hair shone like pure gold, and a crown of violets was on her head. But she was smaller than her father.

Prince Cam fell in love with her immediately, and began to weep. "Alas, that nature has made us so unlike!" he said. "Without you I can never be happy."

The king laughed and stamped his foot. Instantly he grew to be a tall man, and the princess herself was almost as large as Prince Cam, and more beautiful than ever.

"Fairies can be any size they like," the king said. "I appeared small and weak that I might discover whether your heart was really good."

The fairy princess had long loved Prince Cam in secret, and blushed with pleasure when she learned why she had been summoned. The wedding was celebrated with great magnificence, all the people rejoiced, and the fairies came and danced in honor of the good Prince.

Boorum Boola and his son and all their worthless followers were never heard of again. As to the tiger, he was made Grand Vizir, and performed the duties of that post with great credit and dignity.

And Prince Cam and his beautiful bride lived many years, and never knew sickness or sorrow.